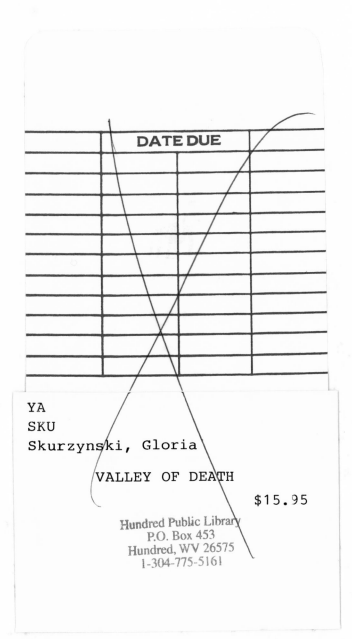

MYSTERIES
IN OUR NATIONAL PARKS

VALLEY OF DEATH

GLORIA SKURZYNSKI AND ALANE FERGUSON

NATIONAL GEOGRAPHIC SOCIETY

WASHINGTON, D.C.

For Suzanne Patrick Fonda,

a great editor and a cherished friend

Text copyright © 2002 Gloria Skurzynski and Alane Ferguson
Cover illustration copyright © 2002 Loren Long

Map by Carl Mehler, Director of Maps
Map research and production by Matt Chwastyk
and Thomas L. Gray

Desert bighorn sheep art by Joan Wolbier

This is a work of fiction. Any resemblance to living persons or events other than descriptions of natural phenomena is purely coincidental.

Library of Congress Cataloging-in-Publication Data

Skurzynski, Gloria.
  Valley of death / by Gloria Skurzynski and Alane Ferguson.
     p. cm. — (Mysteries in our national parks ; #8)
Summary: The Landon family makes a trip to Death Valley
National Park accompanied by a mysterious new foster child,
fourteen-year-old Leesa Sherman.
  ISBN 0-7922-6698-6 (Hardcover)
  ISBN 0-7922-6699-4 (Paperback)
  [1. Death Valley National Park (Calif. and Nev.) 2. National
parks and reserves. 3. Foster home care—Fiction. 4. Mystery and
detective stories.] I. Ferguson, Alane. II. Title. III. Series.
  PZ7.S6287 Val 2002
  [Fic]—dc21
                                        2001003618

Printed in the United States of America

ACKNOWLEDGMENTS

The authors are grateful for the valuable information

provided so generously by the staff at Death Valley

National Park, especially Linda W. Greene, Chief,

Division of Resources Management; Tim Stone,

Management Assistant; Hank Kodele, Law

Enforcement Ranger; Nancy R. Wizner, Assistant

Chief Ranger; Alan Van Walkenburg, Interpretive

Ranger; and Dick Anderson, Naturalist.

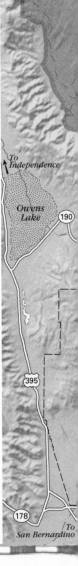

PARK DATA

States: California and Nevada

Established: as a National Monument, 1933;
as a National Park, 1994

Area: 3.37 million acres

Extremes: Highest recorded temperature in
North America (134°F); Lowest point in North
America (282 feet below sea level); Driest place in
North America (1.92 inches, average annual rainfall)

Natural Features: Extensive dune fields,
salt flats, and fossil deposits; a volcanic crater 600-feet
deep; hot springs; and bristlecone pine forests

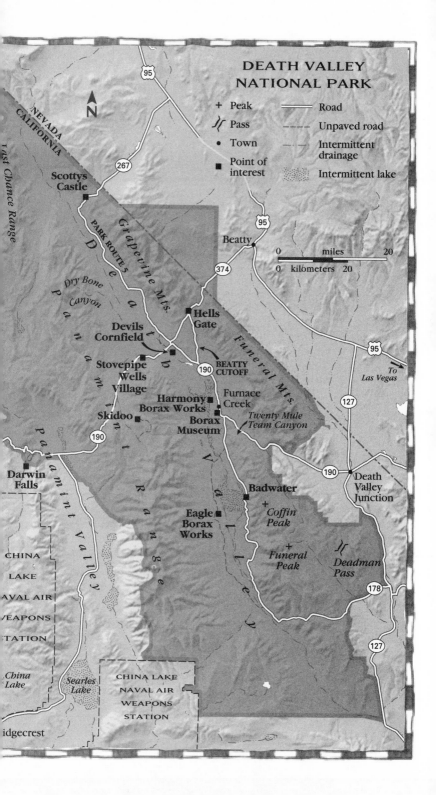

He'd been hiding in an abandoned mine shaft, but now it was time for action. The sand whipped his eyes, almost blinding him, but in the distance he could see the girl. She seemed to be searching for something. Good. That meant her guard would be down. If he were careful, she wouldn't see him until it was too late.

Circling so that he approached from behind, he poised to strike. In his camouflage fatigues he blended into his surroundings as if he were a ghost. But he was a ghost who could kill. With a .45-caliber Magnum strapped beneath his fatigue jacket and an eight-inch army knife hidden in his boot, no one had better try to stop him.

Dropping onto the sand, he radioed to his commander, "I see the subject at oh-two-hundred hours. She appears to be alone. What are my orders?"

"Get her. Now."

CHAPTER ONE

Eerie organ music filled the room, floating up to the carved wooden rafters. The music rose and fell, chords crashed and thundered, notes soared to trembling trebles and descended to rumbling bass. No human created the music; no fingers struck the ivory keys. With not a soul near the keyboard, the organ played itself. Ghostly! Jack thought. Like so much else in Death Valley.

Like the girl Leesa, who looked ghostly, with her pale face and shadowed eyes. She was the latest of the foster children sheltered by the Landon family, and for the first time, Jack knew nothing about her. Always before, his mother and father had told Jack and his sister, Ashley, just why each foster child had come to them, why the child required temporary care, and how long he or she would be likely to stay. But not this time. For some reason, Jack's parents wouldn't say anything about Leesa Sherman, except that she was 14 years old and she needed a safe haven.

Abruptly, the organ recital ended. It seemed strange to applaud a mechanical organ that no one had actually played, but everyone did it anyway. "Wasn't that cool, Jack?" Ashley asked. "It was so spooky—I mean, seeing those keys go up and down all by themselves."

Before Jack had a chance to answer, the tour guide announced, "This was the final stop on our tour of Scotty's Castle, or Death Valley Ranch, as the real owner called it. You may exit through this door. Be careful going down the stairs."

The four Landons—mother Olivia, father Steven, Jack, and Ashley—held open the heavy door for one another and for Leesa. Just as they reached the staircase that descended to the courtyard of this unlikely desert castle, chimes began to ring in the clock tower.

"Bong, bong, bong," Ashley intoned with the chimes. "Three o'clock, Mom. I'm hungry, and there's a refreshment stand right over there. Can I buy a smoothie?"

"Not now, honey," Olivia answered. "We need to get to Furnace Creek Ranch, and that's another hour's drive, or maybe even longer on these two-lane roads. After we're registered and settled in our rooms, we'll have dinner."

The Landons, plus Leesa, had flown from Jackson Hole, Wyoming, to Las Vegas, Nevada, where they'd rented a Toyota Land Cruiser for the two-and-a-half hour drive to Death Valley National Park. Entering the park right at the California-Nevada state line, they'd come upon Scotty's Castle, an architectural marvel sprouting so unexpectedly in the bleak desert that they just had to stop for a tour. Designed by a millionaire in the 1930s, the buildings were amazing enough— stucco walls, red-tile roofs, the clock tower, and a Moorish-style minaret. Inside, the castle held even more surprises: Expensively furnished rooms with hollow walls cooled by flowing water, so that in the summer, when the temperature in Death Valley itself reached 120 degrees, Scotty's Castle was a bearable 85 degrees.

Throughout the tour, Leesa had stayed silent. In fact, she'd been silent since she came to the Landons two days earlier. If anyone asked her something, like, "Would you like another glass of milk?" she'd answer yes or no. But she never spoke up on her own, not even to say, "Pass the salt."

Leesa, the mystery girl. Ashley hadn't been able to get any information out of her, and Ashley could usually soften up the toughest foster kids. Funny, even though Leesa was 14 and Ashley was only 11, they looked a lot alike—petite, with matching dark hair that Leesa wore in one long braid and Ashley tied back with a scrunchie into a thick ponytail.

Then—surprise!—Leesa asked a question. Almost in a whisper, she inquired, "How did that organ play like that, all by itself?"

Jack's father answered, "Ever hear of a player piano? It uses a paper roll with little holes in it, one for each key of music. The organ works the same way, but since it has more than a thousand organ pipes hidden behind the wall, the sound can get pretty powerful compared to a player piano. Did you enjoy it, Leesa?"

All the Landons turned toward Leesa, waiting for her answer. She must have used up all the words she was planning to spend right then, because she just nodded. After a minute, Jack's mother said, "Well then, let's all get into the Land Cruiser and drive to Furnace Creek."

What a name—Furnace Creek! As Jack studied the park map, he found other names that sounded just as harsh: Badwater, Last Chance Range, Deadman Pass, Funeral Mountains, Coffin Peak, Dry Bone Canyon, Hells Gate, Devils Cornfield—place-names that wouldn't exactly tempt a person to visit Death Valley. But the Landons hadn't come on vacation; they were there because Olivia Landon—*Doctor* Olivia Landon, wildlife veterinarian—had been called to help solve the mysterious deaths of the park's desert bighorn sheep.

Once they drove past the leafy green trees and date palms and Joshua trees that surrounded the oasis of Scotty's Castle, the Landons found themselves in the real Death Valley, the hottest, deepest, and driest place in the U.S.A. They passed miles of desert sand decorated with nothing more than rocks and saltbrush and creosote bushes. Then, ahead of them in all that desolation, something raced across the road.

"What was that?" Ashley cried. "Stop, Dad!"

Steven pulled to the shoulder of the highway just as Jack said, "It's a coyote. Look, he's standing right there, staring at us."

Like a welcoming committee, the coyote faced them, his eyes focusing on the Landons in their vehicle, his big ears straight up like radar.

"What a beautiful specimen!" Olivia exclaimed. "That's just about the healthiest coyote I've ever seen."

"Let me grab my camera," Steven said, but Jack had already reached into the tailgate to pass his dad's camera case forward.

The coyote's ears moved forward and then back, as though trying to pick up a signal. His coat—tawny on the head and back, cream-colored on the face and underside—shone thick and full, and rippled slightly in the desert breeze. When he turned in profile, as though posing for Steven's camera, they saw his tail, hanging long, thick, and bushy.

"He's licking his lips like he's hungry," Ashley said. "Since he looks so big and strong, he must find plenty of rats and mice and stuff to eat out here in the desert."

Olivia answered, "I have a suspicion that the exact opposite is true. The way he's acting—standing right there, not moving, not the least afraid of us humans—makes me think he's a little beggar looking for people food. He probably hangs around the road all day waiting for tourists' cars, and I'll bet half the visitors who see him open their car windows and throw him a cookie or peanuts or whatever they have." Olivia shook her head. "It's a bad, bad situation when wild animals become dependent on handouts."

Jack remembered Glacier National Park, where grizzly bears fed by tourists would invade campgrounds to look for food, causing trouble for themselves *and* the visitors. And Hawaii Volcanoes National Park, where the néné—geese that had almost become extinct—often got run over when they approached cars for handouts. Neither Jack nor Ashley would ever think of feeding wildlife, no matter how tame the animals appeared to be. They'd had that lesson drummed into them by their parents since they were little.

In a soft voice, Leesa murmured, "My dad says coyotes are varmints and all varmints deserve to be shot."

For a moment everyone stayed silent, surprised by Leesa's comment. Then, gently, Olivia asked, "Do you believe that too, Leesa?"

"I—don't know." Her deep-set, shadowed eyes lowered to stare at the floor. "I'm just saying what my dad thinks."

Jack had heard it before, that wolves, coyotes, bobcats, and mountain lions were useless predators that harmed cattle and sheep and sometimes carried off little children—that part of it certainly wasn't true. "Our mom and dad teach us," he told Leesa, "that every living creature has its own value, its own reason for being on Earth."

Jack was in the backseat next to the open window, with Ashley between him and Leesa. Touching Leesa's hand, Ashley asked, "You wouldn't want to shoot something as beautiful as that coyote, would you?"

Leesa hesitated, then shook her head.

Starting the engine, Steven said, "We'd better get going. Jack, put my camera back—carefully—where you got it. It's close to four o'clock now, and I want to have us settled at the ranch in plenty of time to set up for pictures. I've heard that the sunsets are spectacular here at Death Valley." Steven, a professional photographer, usually shot pictures of wildlife, but he was always ready to photograph anything else that attracted him.

Throughout the rest of the drive, Ashley kept talking about the animals they'd seen at the national parks they'd visited and how each one had its place in the ecosystem. Then she started on the scenery they were driving past. "Look at this desert," she said to Leesa. "Some people might think it's ugly because there aren't any green trees or flowing streams, but to me it has its own kind of beauty. Like the colors in the rocks. The ripples in the sand...."

Leesa no longer seemed to listen. She stared out through her own window toward the Grapevine Mountains in the distance, dark, sculpted, limestone rock streaked with white calcite. What a strange girl, Jack thought. Where did she come from, and why was she with them? He wished his parents would fill him in on Leesa's background, but they were as silent about Leesa as Leesa was silent by choice. She didn't respond at all to Ashley's nonstop chattering.

Once more they emerged from sandy desert into an astonishing oasis of grass and palm trees and—a golf course! "This is where we're staying," Steven announced. "Furnace Creek Ranch." Before he finished speaking, a horse-drawn wagon rounded a corner and headed straight toward them.

"Pull over!" Olivia told Steven, and then, laughing, added, "I think horses must have the right of way."

It was an authentic, old-fashioned buckboard wagon, the kind people used for transportation a long time ago. Two patient horses pulled the wagon that rolled along on tall, metal-spoked wheels. Even though the Cruiser's windows were closed, Jack could hear the *clop, clop, clop* of the horses' hooves. The driver raised his whip in a salute to the Landons—or maybe he was warning them to stay on their own side of the road.

As they swerved to the right, the Cruiser hit a speed bump, knocking Leesa into Ashley. "Sorry," Leesa said, and giggled a little, the first time Jack had heard anything like laughter coming from her.

When they finally found their rooms and got all their luggage inside, they discovered that their sliding doors opened right onto the golf course. "Hey, I could go out scouting for lost balls and sell them back to the golfers," Jack joked.

"Check over there in front of the golf course," Ashley said. "It's a stable. That's where all the horses are. Can we go riding, Mom? Please?"

"It's too late now," Olivia answered, "and I don't know what my schedule will be like tomorrow. But it sure is perfect weather for riding."

Luckily for the Landons, they were visiting Death Valley during the mild month of February rather than in the searing heat of summer, when hiking became dangerous and tourists often got into trouble. As always, when the family traveled during the school year, the kids had to bring along their homework and write papers about the park and its flora and fauna. That was an easy price to pay for the chance to see some of the greatest scenery in the United States.

"Which room is mine?" Leesa asked, picking up the shopping bag that held her clothes.

"Ours, you mean," Ashley answered. "Whenever our foster kid—uh, I mean, our guest—is a boy, he shares a room with Jack, and I sleep on a cot in Mom and Dad's room. If the guest is a girl, we share a room, and Jack stays with Mom and Dad. So you and I will bunk together while we're here, Leesa."

"Don't worry, Ashley doesn't snore—at least not too loud," Jack teased.

Ashley punched him in the arm, but Leesa didn't even smile. She just stared through the window at the gathering darkness.

CHAPTER TWO

"What the heck is borax?" Jack asked. "I keep seeing it on the map: Eagle Borax Works Ruins, Borax Museum, Harmony Borax Works, Twenty Mule Team Borax...."

Jack, Ashley, and Leesa were wandering through a collection of old wagons, machinery, and an actual locomotive on display in the Furnace Creek Ranch complex. In the restaurant nearby, Steven and Olivia still lingered over their breakfast coffee—Jack could see them through the window, their heads close together, talking.

"Jack, if you'd bought the booklet in the museum like I did, you wouldn't have to ask," Ashley said. "It only cost me a dollar."

"Why should I waste my money buying one when you already did? So tell me what borax is."

Leafing through the pages, Ashley answered, "It says here that borax aids digestion, keeps milk sweet, gets rid of dandruff, improves your complexion, cures epilepsy, dissolves bunions—"

"Give me a break!" Jack hooted. "Nothing could do all that."

Ashley laughed. "That's what people were saying about it back in 1890. Too bad you can't get some for your complexion, Jack. I noticed that zit on your cheek…."

Jack grabbed the booklet and swatted Ashley with it, but it was too flimsy to have any effect. Then he opened it and got interested in the story of borax, a white mineral mined in Death Valley. The best part was about the 20-mule teams—actually 9 pairs of mules and a pair of horses—all lined up with a 120-foot-long chain running down the middle of them. The chain connected the team to two huge wagon loads of borax, plus a big iron water tank, with the entire load totaling 36 tons. Jack could imagine those poor mules hauling all that weight out of the valley in the boiling heat of summer. Even worse, sometimes the brakes on the wagons would fail, and the heavy load would thunder downhill on top of the panic-stricken mules trying to stay ahead of it.

"Hey! Give me back my book," Ashley demanded.

Since Jack was now five feet seven inches tall, he had no trouble holding the book too high for his shrimpy little sister to reach. She kept jumping up to slap at his arm.

"Leesa, come help me," Ashley begged, but Leesa didn't want to get involved in a sibling tussle. She backed away to stand in front of one of the huge, old borax wagons on display in front of the ranch. Leesa was short to begin with, not much taller than Ashley, and next to the seven-foot-high rear wheel of the wagon, she looked like a Munchkin.

"Here, take your book," Jack said, stuffing it down the back of Ashley's T-shirt. "Mom and Dad are coming." Sometimes, if he teased his sister a little too much, Jack got in trouble with his parents. Usually Ashley didn't tell on him, though. She was pretty cool that way. Pretending to be serious, he said, "As I was mentioning, today borax is used to make glass and soap and certain cosmetics, which, by the way, I saw you sneaking out of Mom's purse—"

"*What* cosmetics!"

"Her lipstick. I don't think there's borax in that."

"I put it right back," Ashley said quickly, blushing a little. "OK, we're even now. You don't tell Mom about the lipstick, and I won't mention your zit again. Truce?"

"Deal." They gave each other a high five.

By then Steven and Olivia had reached them. "Did you see all the old mining equipment behind the Borax Museum?" Steven asked. "Back in those days, they made machinery large and heavy to do big jobs. It took a lot of muscle power to move those loads."

"We'll come back and spend some time here later," Olivia told them. "Right now I have a meeting at the visitor center. Unless the rest of you would rather stay here, and I can go the visitor center by myself...."

"We've seen this," Jack told her. "There's probably other good stuff at the visitor center."

When they got there, Olivia went into one of the offices in the back, while Steven headed straight for the photo books of Death Valley. Ashley started chatting up one of the interpretive rangers, and Jack was left with Leesa.

Silent as always, she at least walked next to him as they wandered past the displays of Indian artifacts and baskets. At the end of a large room they came to a glass case holding what a sign identified as a desert bighorn sheep, now mounted and on display. Its enormous horns curved in an almost perfect circle from the top of its head to beneath its jaws.

"That's why we're here," Jack said, trying to start a conversation.

"Why?"

"Because my mother is a wildlife veterinarian, so when the national parks have problems with any of their wildlife, they call my mother as a consultant. Here in Death Valley, some bighorn sheep have died, and no one knows why. Just a few died, but there aren't that many living in the park, and park officials don't want to lose any of them. The sheep stay high up in the mountains."

"Oh," Leesa said.

Great conversation. Well, he tried.

A while later, while Leesa was studying a chart that showed how far below sea level different parts of the park were, Ashley came up to Jack and whispered, "Did you find out anything?

"About Leesa? No. She doesn't talk."

"She talks," Ashley said. "I mean, she talked to me a little bit last night when we were alone in the room. I think I figured out why she's with us."

"Tell me," Jack demanded. It bothered him when his sister knew something that he didn't.

Pulling him into a corner of the room, Ashley said softly, "It's really romantic, like Romeo and Juliet. She's in love with this boy, a ninth grader like she is. His name is Aaron. Well, she didn't really say they were in love, she just said they were very good friends."

"So?"

"So Leesa's family doesn't like this boy's family, and when her dad found a note Aaron had written to her, he got so mad that he wouldn't let Leesa go to school for three whole weeks!"

"Wow! What did the note say?"

"Nothing, really," Ashley answered. "Aaron was just asking her to go to a movie with him. Then, after she missed all those weeks of school, the principal found out it was her father who was keeping her at home, and he called Social Services. That's why she's here with us now, I guess, until things get straightened out with her father."

Jack was puzzled by that. Lots of people pulled their kids out of the public schools for one reason or another. Home schooling was pretty common in Wyoming. And why would his parents be so secretive about Leesa if that's all there was to the story?

Olivia came up to them then and announced, "I have five free hours, so we can go exploring. Since the biologists are waiting for a blood test to come back on one of the sheep that died, there's no sense for us to keep speculating on the cause of death until the test results arrive by FedEx this afternoon at three o'clock. So where would you like to go?"

"Skidoo!" Ashley yelled so loudly that some German tourists turned to stare at her. She clapped her hands over her mouth, then said more quietly, "I've been talking to that ranger, and he told me all about this old ghost town called Skidoo. I really want to see it, Mom. We can get there and back in five hours, no problem."

"Fine with me," Olivia answered. "I'll check with your father."

Olivia didn't think to ask Leesa whether she would be interested in seeing a ghost town. It was easy to overlook Leesa, since she always seemed to melt into the shadows. To be polite, Jack said, "How about you, Leesa? Would you like to see Skidoo?" Leesa just shrugged, which maybe meant "OK" or just "I don't care" or "whatever."

Once again the five of them were back in the Land Cruiser, this time with Leesa in the middle of the backseat between Jack and Ashley. She sat stiffly, being super careful that not a single part of her would brush against Jack, not even the edge of her sneaker. Jack had the feeling that if she'd had room to move even farther away from him, she'd have jumped at the chance. Not that he was at all anxious to make contact with this girl. Leesa was a high-school freshman who probably considered Jack, an eighth grader, far down on the social scale. Besides, she already had a boyfriend, named Aaron. Not that *Jack* would ever want to be her boyfriend….

His thoughts were interrupted by his mother, who turned to tell them, "This morning I found out something that's going to interest you, but first I want to give you some background information."

Trust their mother to create a buildup like that and then make them wait for the exciting part. "Go ahead," Jack said.

"As you know," Olivia began, "I'm here because a few desert bighorn sheep have died mysteriously. There were no outside signs of trauma on the sheep, so we're suspecting it might have been something they ate, or an infection transmitted to them from some other animal. Sheep are fairly sensitive to diseases from other species."

Ashley leaned forward, interested, as always, in endangered wildlife. Leesa stared straight ahead.

"They found three sheep that had been dead long enough that not much remained of the carcasses—it takes no more than two days for even a large carcass like a sheep's to be picked clean, down to the skeleton, by coyotes or ravens or mountain lions or all of the above. But they found one sheep in the throes of death, and were able to get a blood sample before it died. That's what I'm waiting for—the analysis of that blood sample."

Olivia seemed to be taking longer than usual to reach the point, but from the look on her face, she was getting closer.

"Well, now," she said, "bighorn sheep don't have many real enemies, but they do have competitors for food and water—the burros."

"You mean like the gold miners brought in a long time ago?" Ashley chimed in. "The ranger was telling me all about them. When the mines ran out and the miners gave up and went home, they left their burros behind, here in Death Valley."

"Right. And the burros multiplied and multiplied and multiplied some more until there were several thousand of them in and around Death Valley. They're tough, feisty little critters that can live in a climate like this, but when there got to be so many of them, they ruined the area for the bighorn sheep. The burros trample vegetation and pollute the water supply."

Jack thought his mother should have been a school-teacher. Nothing delighted her more than explaining things to kids, especially if the subject happened to be animals. Her eyes would light up, and she'd make everything come alive. But maybe that was because she was talking about animals—her real love.

When Olivia handled any species—dogs or wolves, elk or deer, horses or even manatees—her touch was expert and yet gentle. It was as though animals knew they could put their trust in her. And so did the foster kids who stayed with the Landons. They found Olivia sympathetic and understanding.

She continued, "Since burros are exotic animals—" Olivia interrupted herself to explain to Leesa, "That means they aren't native to Death Valley. And because they had a bad impact on the ecosystem and the desert bighorn sheep, National Park policy decreed that the burros had to go."

"How'd they get rid of them?" Jack wanted to know.

A shadow crossed Olivia's face. "A lot of them were removed by direct reduction. That's a polite way of saying they were shot. Others were trapped and removed. Then, in the 1980s, the park joined with the

Bureau of Land Management in an Adopt-a-Burro program. People could adopt them and take them home to ride, or for work, or just for pets—but not, heaven forbid, to sell to slaughterhouses."

Leesa moved forward, listening intently.

"How'd they get the burros, Mom?" Ashley asked. "Did they come here to the park and say, 'You! The brown burro with the big ears. I'll take you.'"

Steven laughed at that. "I wish it was that easy. I used to round up horses when I lived on a ranch, and they never moved along without an argument."

In Zion National Park, Jack had watched his father capture a wild horse, but that wouldn't have qualified as a roundup. "Is that how they get the burros for adoption?" he asked. "They round them up?"

"Uh-huh. Of course, they can't capture all of them that way," Olivia explained. "The ones that live way up in the mountains may be too hard to reach and—well, sometimes they still have to rely on direct reduction."

"Shooting," Leesa murmured.

"It's an emotional issue that nobody likes to deal with," Olivia explained, "but you have to realize that wild burros tend to damage the environment pretty badly, especially for the bighorn sheep...." Then Olivia brightened. "But wild burro roundups save the lives of anywhere from two to three hundred burros a year. And guess when the next wild burro roundup is going to happen—right here in the park. The day after tomorrow!"

She'd finally made it to the exciting part, and it really had been worth the wait. That is, if—"Will we still be here? Where in the park? Can we watch it?" Jack and Ashley demanded, peppering their mother with questions.

"Yes, we'll still be here, and to your last question, maybe," Olivia answered. "Or maybe not. These roundups are carefully organized by the park and the BLM, with trained wranglers and helicopters that herd the burros down from the mountains and into corrals. Still, if we're real lucky, and if we promise to stay far out of the way—" She turned farther in her seat to ask, "Would you like that, Leesa?"

Leesa's expression was hard to read. "Yesterday," she began, "Jack and Ashley said that every living creature on Earth has value. Now you just told us that park rangers used to shoot wild burros. So if it's wrong to kill coyotes, why wasn't it wrong to kill burros?"

The silence that followed was broken only when Olivia murmured, "It's complicated. Coyotes are native to the park. They've always been here. Burros were brought here. They are the outsiders, and the Park Service feels that exotic species need to be removed."

"I just don't see why there always have to be two different sets of rules for everything," Leesa told them. "I'm never sure which one is right."

"It isn't two different sets of rules," Olivia explained. "It's one environmental policy. The Park Service has been given a mandate to preserve and protect certain areas of our country for all Americans to enjoy. That means these areas must be kept exactly as nature created them. Nature didn't intend for burros to live in Death Valley. They're interlopers—outsiders. They have to be removed, but the removal is carried out in the most humane way possible."

Leesa didn't look convinced.

CHAPTER THREE

Peering through the window, Jack stared across the barren valley floor toward the Funeral Mountains in the distance. What would it be like to get lost in that wilderness, to wander without food or water—no, food wouldn't really be a problem. Before a person could starve to death, he'd die of dehydration.

The thought of wandering in the desert reminded Jack of the gift he'd received from his parents a few months before on his 13th birthday—a perfect present, considering all the traveling his family did to the different national parks. He grabbed his backpack, opened it, and took out one half of the gift. It felt good in his hands, with a nice heft to it. After he pressed the button that turned it on, he sat watching the little red light that pulsed on and off like the beacon on top of a police car.

"What's that thing?" Leesa asked.

"A two-way radio. Which means there needs to be another one just like it for it to work, and I have it somewhere in here…the other…," he said, rummaging again in his backpack, "…unit."

It might have been his imagination, but it seemed that Leesa cringed when he said the word "unit." She sure was impossible to figure out. Oh well….

"Here it is. Now I'll show you how these work," he said, and tossed the second radio to Ashley. "Face the window, Ashley, and I'll do the same on my side, then we'll talk real low."

Ashley caught the handheld radio, then, turning it on, she whispered into it, "Go ahead, Jack, say something. Over."

Jack pushed down the talk button on his unit and whispered back, "Can you hear me? Over."

"I can hear both of you whispering anyway, so what's the point," Leesa said, unimpressed.

"Mmm, this isn't a very good test," Jack answered defensively. "If we were out in the open, we could talk into this thing and hear each other up to two miles away. Wait till we stop somewhere, and we'll give you a better demonstration."

From the front seat, Steven said, "How about if we stop here to look at those sand dunes? I want to get some pictures."

"OK, but not too long," Olivia told him. "If we're

going to reach Skidoo, we need to get there and be able to drive back in time for my meeting."

The dunes were worth the stop. From a distance they looked like Egyptian pyramids: golden peaks, with flat sides rising and then narrowing to a point. Closer, they turned out to be huge heaps of sand sculpted by desert winds. "I'm going out to the closest dune," Jack said, "so I can show Leesa how these two-way radios really work."

"You better not, Jack—you're supposed to stay on marked trails in the national parks, and there aren't any marked trails here," Ashley warned him.

"In this case it's allowed," Steven said. "Wind constantly reshapes the dunes, so footprints left behind by hikers get blown away before the day's end. Go ahead, Jack. Walk out there so you'll give some perspective to my pictures of the dunes."

"But make it quick, please," Olivia told him.

Jack tried to run fast, but running in sand was like being in a dream where you want to get away from something that's chasing you, but you can only move in slow motion. With every step he kept sinking into the soft sand; finally, after he'd gone about a hundred yards, he gave up. "Ashley, do you read me?" he asked into the radio.

"Read you loud and clear. Say something else, and I'll let Leesa hold this handset so she can hear you, too." In the distance, he could see Ashley hand the radio to Leesa, instructing her to press the button while she spoke into it.

"Hi, Leesa," he said. "I have sand in my shoes."

"I heard that," Leesa answered. "This thing's really cool. But your mother says you're supposed to come back here."

"Be right there. Over and out."

At the Land Cruiser, as Jack was dumping sand out of his shoes, Steven exclaimed, "Hey, guys, look at those dust devils to the west of us!" Less than a mile ahead of them, wind had whipped sand and dust into half a dozen high whirlwinds that danced on the rim of the hills, all in a row, like a chorus line of phantoms.

"What would it be like in the middle of one of those things?" Ashley asked.

"Hard to breathe," Steven answered. "And you couldn't see much. Dust devils are like little tornadoes, but not as violent. So if you were inside one of those baby twisters, you wouldn't get sucked up like you would in a tornado, but it wouldn't be much fun."

"OK, guys, we better go," Olivia urged. "There's a restaurant up ahead a little way, but if no one's too hungry, I think we ought to keep going and see Ashley's ghost town first, then we can eat on the way back. That way, if we're running late, we'll just pick up a pizza and take it with us."

Since they'd finished breakfast not much more than two hours earlier, everyone agreed to that plan.

The drive was already turning out to be longer than they'd expected, and after another half hour Ashley yelled, "Stop the car!"

"Why? Are we at Skidoo?" Jack wanted to know.

"No, not yet, but Dad—you gotta get a picture of those rocks. Do you see them? They look like ghost heads," Ashley declared. "Like a whole lot of skulls lined up in a haunted house."

Squinting a little, Jack guessed he could see what she was talking about: A thick, dark, craggy layer of rock rested on an almost white layer at the top of a high cliff. The dark rock had eroded into shapes that Ashley, with her big imagination, saw as skulls, probably because shallow caves in the cliff face looked like empty eye sockets above screaming mouths. It would make a great place for a Halloween party.

"Death, death, everywhere you look," Leesa murmured. "This place is depressing."

Since Steven's camera was still on the front seat where he'd put it after photographing the dunes, he picked it up to focus on the ghost heads. Not too far behind them, a person on a motorcycle stopped along the side of the road, probably figuring there must be something worth photographing. That's what happened all the time in the national parks: Someone stopped to take a picture, and it quickly started a chain reaction, every following driver slowing down or stopping to see what was happening. At Yellowstone, if a bear or a moose ambled across a field, traffic could get backed up for a quarter mile.

In a few minutes Steven had taken the pictures Ashley wanted, and they were on their way again. Jack noticed the motorcyclist following, keeping a good distance behind them. He couldn't tell whether it was a man or a woman. Leesa kept turning around to glance at the motorcyclist. Jack wondered why she seemed so interested, but he didn't ask. Maybe she just liked motorcycles.

The drive seemed to go on and on, or maybe it just felt longer because Olivia kept looking at her watch. "According to the map," Jack said, "we ought to be getting close to the turnoff for Skidoo. And there's the sign. Turn left, Dad."

The first hundred yards or so of the dirt road were fairly smooth, but then it turned into a washboard that rattled their teeth. "I hope it's going to be worth it," Ashley said, her voice quavering from the jouncing. "I mean, it's my fault that we're coming way up here on the top of the mountain. The ranger told me it was a special place to visit, but I—I hope—"

"Don't worry about it, sweetie," Steven told her. "I'm looking forward to it because I've never photographed a ghost town before. Hey, maybe I can get a picture of a real ghost."

"Then you could sell it to the *National Enquirer*," Jack answered. "It would rate the front page."

Since the vehicle's jouncing made their voices jiggle, no one said much more until they rounded a curve in the road and came upon the ruins of the ghost town—although the only ruins they could see were old mine structures, with their walls collapsed and their boards faded or fallen down on the slopes. No houses, no stores, no sign at all of the thousands of people who'd once staked their lives and fortunes on hopes of striking gold in these mountains.

"This is it?" Jack asked. He wondered why they'd bothered coming here. There wasn't much to see. He started to walk along the pebbly, sandy, barren surface, and accidentally kicked a rusty tin can. When he reached the place a few yards ahead where the can had landed, he stopped to pick it up.

It was bent in the middle, squeezed into an uneven oval shape—the dusty inside coated with a residue of sand; the outside mottled with colors from copper to rust to the hue of dried blood. As Jack held the dented old can in his hand, scenes began to take shape in his mind. Some old miner must have opened this long ago—maybe a hundred years ago—to eat the beans inside. With pick and shovel, the man had dug inside the earth, hoping his miner's lamp would catch a flash of gold in the rock that surrounded him. Sweating, cursing the heat, drinking lukewarm water from a bucket, he'd have swung that pick again and again, waiting for good fortune to shower down on him.

At the end of long hours of digging, he'd have gone home to a shack or a tent and opened a can of beans for his supper. This can.

"Can I have that?" Ashley asked. "If I tell you a story about Skidoo, and about the ghost that lives here, will you give me the can?"

"No, you can't have it," he told her. "It's like anything else in a national park—you leave things where you find them. I'm putting it back."

Leesa, who'd overheard them, said, "You know a story about this place, Ashley? I'd like to hear it."

By tradition, Ashley was the family storyteller. Before they visited each national park, she'd check out library books to learn all she could about the place. Once they reached the park, she would talk to park rangers, asking questions. They always seemed glad to share stories about park history or about their own personal experiences, like the ranger in Glacier National Park who'd told about her terrifying encounter with a grizzly bear.

Steven climbed next to an old wooden platform that must have been used for who knows what in the gold-mining operation. After setting up his tripod, he started shooting pictures, pointing the lens toward the wave after wave of lavender-hued mountain ranges that stretched in the distance.

"OK, everyone, it's story time," Ashley announced. "I'm going to tell this exactly the way the ranger told it to me. *More or less.* I'll try to remember his words, but I might end up adding just a few of my own— for artistic effect."

"Oh yeah, sure," Jack hooted. "Artistic effect."

"Jack, kindly keep your comments to yourself," Ashley ordered, giving him a look. "First, I'm going to tell you about the name Skidoo. The man who started this town bought up 23 gold mining claims here for $23,000. When he told his wife about it, she said, 'Twenty-three skidoo.'"

"Huh?" Jack and Leesa both stared at Ashley, who'd risen to stand like a performer in front of them. "What's that supposed to mean?" they asked her.

"Back in 1906, when the town got started, 'twenty-three skidoo' was a popular expression that meant 'scram.' The ranger said there might have been other reasons for the name, too, because the town had 23 city blocks, and they had to pipe water about 23 miles from springs at Telescope Peak all the way to Skidoo. It took them a year and a half to lay the water pipes, and lots of men and mules died from working in the heat, while other men just threw down their shovels and quit, leaving their burros behind to wander around the mountains here at Death Valley."

After that rush of words, Ashley took a deep breath. "Now, no more interruptions, Jack. Pay attention. This is a scary ghost story." Looking mysterious, she drew out the word "ghost" until it slowly melted into the word "story." Then she added, "And the best part is that it really happened! It's all true."

Like an actress priming herself for an important stage role, Ashley raised her head, pushed her hair back with both hands, closed her eyes, and took a deep breath.

"Oh, come on," Jack said. "Don't be such a drama queen. If you're going to tell a story, just tell it!"

"Let her do it her own way," Leesa said, softly.

Girls! Jack thought. They always stick together.

CHAPTER FOUR

Gold! Gold was everywhere, some of it lying right on top of the ground, waiting for someone to shovel it up. By the spring of 1907, so many miners had flocked into Skidoo, they figured the population would reach 10,000 before long. Skidoo was on its way to being a real city, with honky-tonks and bathtubs and telegraph wires.

As the town grew, miners hammered together rickety wooden cabins or lived in tents close enough to the gold mine that they wouldn't waste time getting there. All of them itched to make a big strike—fast! To be the first ones to hit that thick vein of gold ore. Surely the very next swing of their picks would uncover riches beyond imagining.

Two men from Wyoming arrived to set up the Skidoo News, *the first newspaper ever printed in Death Valley.*

A banker showed up with $2,000 in his suitcase, and in a corner of the town's grocery store he established the Southern California Bank of Skidoo. Water from mountain springs finally started to flow through that long, long pipeline to quench the thirst of the citizens and run the mining machinery. Skidoo even had entertainment—a herd of trained goats and a troupe of educated fleas.

But not everything was rosy in Skidoo. A man named Hootch Simpson liked to roar around town menacing people with his guns. The citizens of Skidoo—who called themselves Skidoovians—considered Hootch a trouble-maker, a rascal, a scoundrel, and a dirty dog.

One day in April of 1908, Hootch Simpson entered that bank in the corner of the grocery store. He told the banker to hand over $20. The banker said that Hootch didn't have that much in his bank account, but Hootch yelled, "I don't care. I want it anyhow." When he didn't get the money, he made such a huge fuss that the grocery store owner, whose name was Jim Arnold, threw him out of the place.

Three hours passed. Hootch visited a saloon, where he got madder and madder. Soon he went back to the store and said to the owner, "Jim, what do you have against me?"

Jim Arnold answered, "Hootch, I have nothing against you except that when you've been drinking, you are intensely ugly."

At that, Hootch pulled out his gun and shot Jim Arnold dead.

Now, Jim Arnold was well liked in town, while Hootch Simpson was considered a very bad character. Skidoo was still a frontier town, with no real law enforcement (this was almost a century before Death Valley became a national park.) Soon a group of angry Skidoovians got together and asked one another, "Why should we waste time on a jury trial when we know dang well what the outcome will be? Hootch Simpson, this worthless, no-good snake in the grass, has killed our upstanding citizen Jim Arnold. Hootch is guilty as sin. Let's just put a rope around his neck and hang him!"

So they pulled Hootch out of the makeshift jail and marched him to a telegraph pole, where they hanged him high, leaving him up there long enough to teach a good lesson to any other bad characters who might be tempted to commit a crime in Skidoo. After they cut Hootch down, they decided that a nice burial would be wasted on a scoundrel like him. So they put his body into a cheap coffin made of pine and dumped it into an old mine shaft. There are lots of abandoned mine shafts all around here.

That might have been the end of the story, but it wasn't....

Two hundred miles away, a reporter for the Los Angeles Herald *heard about the shooting—but not about the hanging. He thought he ought to go to Skidoo to cover the trial for his newspaper. The reporter took his camera so he could get some good pictures for his paper, but when he reached Skidoo, he discovered that he'd got there too late. The citizens had taken the law into their own hands and had already hanged Hootch Simpson from the telegraph pole.*

The reporter felt bad that he had missed the big story, and the townspeople felt bad, too, that they'd disappointed a big-city reporter. Then someone had an idea. Why not pull Hootch's coffin out of the mine shaft and hang him again? That way the reporter— who had come all the way from Los Angeles—could get his photographs.

And that's just what they did. For the second time, Hootch Simpson got hanged from a pole, even though he was already dead. The happy reporter took his photographs and returned to Los Angeles.

And that might have been the end of the story. But it wasn't....

The town doctor, whose name was McDonald, became curious about Hootch Simpson. What would make a man like Hootch turn so mean and nasty and dangerous, he wondered. To satisfy his curiosity, Dr. McDonald crept out of his house in the middle of the night. At the old mine hole, he pulled up Hootch Simpson's body once more. Then, in the interest of science, Dr. McDonald took Hootch's head home with him to study it. Just the head, that was all. The rest

of Hootch was returned to his grave in the aban-
doned mine shaft.

For years, Dr. McDonald kept Hootch's skull on dis-
play in his office, where any other doctor who was
passing by could examine it. Later, when Skidoo became
a ghost town, the skull disappeared. No one knows
what became of it.

Now, all these years later, Hootch Simpson's ghost
still lives in the old mine shaft—during the day. But
at night it wanders around Skidoo looking for its lost
head. You can hear Hootch moaning and howling
and calling out on the wind, "What do you people have
against me? Give me back my head! Oooooooh! I've
lost my head!"

Jack exclaimed, "That's about the dumbest ghost
story I ever heard."

"Except that it happens to be true," Ashley told
him. "Well, actually, most of it is true, but some parts
of it might not be entirely true since the story got
turned into a legend over the years. But most of it's
true! The ranger told me you can find it in lots of
books. Except…well…." She looked a little sheepish.
"I did make up one small part of it. But I won't tell
you which part."

"That's easy," Jack said. "You made up about
Hootch Simpson wandering around here searching
for his head."

Wrinkling her nose, Ashley said, "What I really think is that he's looking for another head—*anyone's* head! Like yours, Jack."

"Or maybe yours! *Ooooooh,*" Jack moaned, mocking Ashley. "I'm a ghost, and I want Ashley Landon's head." Then, oddly, they did hear a moan, as the desert breeze churned itself into a wind. It blew through the dried-out old boards with a sound like the low notes of a cello. Grains of sand danced across the surface of the ground, raising dust all around.

"Looks like more dust devils might be forming," Steven said. "We'd better get back into the Cruiser."

"Wait, Dad, please," Ashley begged. "Give me a few minutes to really look around, to imagine where everything used to be in the story I just told. I didn't have enough time to see stuff, and I love this old place. I love everything about Death Valley."

"Five minutes," Steven told her. "I'll give you five minutes while I pack up the camera. If this dust gets worse, we might have trouble seeing the road on our way down the mountain."

"Ashley, take one of Jack's two-way radios," Olivia instructed, "and leave the other one here with me. Jack, you go with Ashley."

"Do I have to?" he complained.

"Never mind, I'll go," Leesa said. "I owe her one for telling the story. Only I didn't know it would be so gruesome."

"Thanks, Leesa," Ashley said, grabbing her hand. "Dad, don't start counting the five minutes till we get a head start, OK?"

"I'm starting right now. One Mississippi, two Mississippi…."

Ashley and Leesa dashed off, hand in hand. In her free hand, Ashley waved the yellow-and-black two-way radio to show Olivia that she'd taken it.

When they were gone, Jack helped his father collapse the tripod and blow dust off the camera lenses, then pack them into their cases. "I got a couple good shots of these old mining structures," Steven said. "Good thing I took them before the wind blew up, while the sun was still bright enough to light up the streaks on that weathered wood."

"Whew, this dust!" Olivia exclaimed. "I'm going to get back into the Cruiser. The walkie-talkie will work from inside the car, won't it, Jack?"

"Don't call it a walkie-talkie. That's what they used to be called a long time ago when they didn't work as well. This is a two-way radio, Mom, and yes it will operate from inside the Cruiser. Just remember—push down the button when you want to talk, but don't push any of the other buttons." Jack felt protective of his dual radios, because he knew how expensive they were. He wasn't too happy about Ashley having one of them out there wherever she was, but he supposed she couldn't really hurt it in five minutes.

The wind seemed to be blowing harder, driving grains of sand against Jack's bare legs. He wished he'd worn his jeans, but even in February Death Valley was warm enough for shorts. As Jack and his father opened the Cruiser to put the camera equipment in the tailgate, they could hear Olivia saying, "Your time's almost up, Ashley. You better start back."

Ashley's electronic voice answered, crackling with a lot of static, *"Just one more minute, Mom. I can see something over there, but I'm not sure what it is."*

"Where's Leesa?" Olivia asked into the handset. She waited for half a minute, and when Ashley didn't reply right away, she asked again, "Ashley, can you hear me? I said, where's Leesa?"

Still no reply. Jack came around to the front of the car and told his mother, "You're probably doing something wrong. If you hold down the talk button when the other person is saying something, you won't hear a word."

"I'm not holding down the button. She's just not answering. Ashley, Ashley, do you hear me? Come in, Ashley."

In the moment of silence that followed, Jack said, "Let me try. Ashley Landon, this is your big brother telling you that you better answer—*now!*—because Mom's starting to worry. Over."

Steven said, "If she's not answering, it might mean the batteries have gone dead."

"Impossible, Dad. I put in fresh batteries just before we left home." At that moment they did hear a voice, but it wasn't coming through the two-way radio. The shouts sounded so distant it was hard to tell which direction they came from, especially since the wind made noise blowing through the old rafters.

"Is that Ashley yelling?" Steven asked. After a minute a figure began to appear through the dust, slowly, like a shadow, barely visible at first and then....

"It's Leesa!" Jack yelled. "Ashley must be right behind her." But when Leesa came closer, they could see that she was alone.

"I lost her!" Leesa cried. "She just disappeared! I got a stone in my shoe, and when I stopped to take it out—she was gone!"

Steven shouted, "We'd better find her, fast, before this windstorm gets worse! Jack, keep trying that two-way radio. Olivia, get the binoculars—both pairs. You and I will climb to that rise over there so we can see better. Ashley can't be very far away—she's only been gone a few minutes."

Jack, too, climbed onto higher ground so there'd be less interference while he tried to make contact with the other radio. Speaking with his mouth right next to the little holes that worked like a telephone mouthpiece, he said, "Ashley, come in. Ashley, if you're playing games and jerking us around because of that stupid ghost story, I'm gonna clean your clock good when you get back. And if you've lost my radio handset—"

Leesa told Jack, "She didn't lose it. She was talking into it the last time I saw her."

"So give me an answer, Ashley. Now!" he said. "Mom and Dad are really getting freaked. This isn't funny."

Nothing. Not a word. In a shaking voice, Leesa said, "I'm sorry now I asked her to tell that ghost story. All about death. Maybe this is a bad place."

Soon Jack saw his mother running down the slope toward the Cruiser, which made him think he'd better get down there too. "Come on," he told Leesa. "Looks like something's happening."

Olivia had opened the compartment between the two front seats and was pulling out the Landons' cell phone. She told Jack, "We can't see her anywhere. I'm scared she might have fallen into one of the old mine shafts. I'm calling 911." Since the cell phone was connected to a no-hands speaker, Jack could hear both sides of the conversation:

"This is 911 responding. Please state your name and the nature of your emergency."

"I'm Olivia Landon and my daughter is lost. She's only eleven—"

"Where are you calling from, Ms. Landon?"

"From the old ghost town of Skidoo in Death Valley. Ashley could have fallen into an abandoned mine shaft, and that's why her two-way radio isn't working—"

"Ma'am, you've reached 911 in Inyo County at the Independence, California, center. I'll have to relay your call to the main dispatch in San Bernardino, and they will then call Death Valley National Park, so there's going to be some lag time. I suggest that you dial the Federal Emergency Communications Center directly. I'll give you the number."

"All right, but hurry!" Frantically, Olivia dug through her purse to find a pen and paper. She scribbled down the number, repeated it, and then punched in the numbers again.

By then Steven had reached the Cruiser. "Did you get someone?" he asked.

At the same time Leesa began to sob, "It's all my fault. I should have stayed right beside her."

In the confusion, Jack missed most of what was being said between his mother and the person on the other end of the line, until he heard, *"Stay calm, Mrs. Landon. We'll get a search-and-rescue team there as quickly as possible."*

"Should we start looking in the mine shafts?" Steven shouted into the phone.

The voice answered, *"Definitely not! You don't want to endanger anyone else in your group. The best thing to do is wait there for the search-and-rescue team. Keep your cell phone on so we can communicate with you."*

That made it suddenly real to Jack—Ashley hadn't been joking around. She really was in trouble! His two-way radio handset had fallen out of the car into the dirt. As he picked it up and rubbed it against his T-shirt to clean it, he thought at first that he was still hearing the voice from the emergency number his mother had called. Then he realized that the two-way radio in his hand had begun to crackle with static. "Mom, Dad!" he yelled. "I think it's Ashley."

Instead, it was a rough male voice. *"We have your daughter,"* the voice said.

There must be some mistake, Jack thought, someone else getting on the line from another channel. As he turned up the volume, the voice repeated.

"We have Ashley Landon, and we'll keep her until Leesa Sherman is returned to us. Do not call the police. Understand? Do not call the police."

CHAPTER FIVE

They established a command post in the ranger station at Stovepipe Wells, halfway between Skidoo and Furnace Creek. By the time the Landons got there, three Park Service law-enforcement vehicles had already parked outside, their red and blue beacon lights flashing. The dust storm hadn't amounted to much; just a few dust devils and then it was gone.

"Come inside," a park ranger named Hank told them, and led them to a crowded office in the back of the building. "We've alerted every ranger in the park. They'll stop any vehicle that looks suspicious." Picking up a notepad, he said, "First, let me get all your names."

"Steven and Olivia Landon," Steven said, pointing to himself and his wife. "This is our son, Jack, and this is Leesa Sherman."

"I guess she's the girl the unknown man said he wanted in exchange for your daughter, Ashley, right? Have you heard any more from him?"

"No."

"Has your two-way radio been turned on the whole time?"

"Yes."

"I think you'd better fill me in on everything from the beginning," Hank told them. "There's enough chairs; go ahead, folks, sit down."

The ranger stood facing them. A thick leather belt around his waist held a .40-caliber handgun, pepper spray, handcuffs, a baton for subduing any assailant that got close enough, a flashlight, and extra ammunition. This was an officer prepared for any kind of duty. "Why don't you start by telling me about Leesa?" he suggested.

This time no one noticed or seemed to care that Jack could hear everything being said. "Her father is a member of a militia group called The Unit," Steven began, his voice tight with strain.

The Unit! Jack remembered Leesa's reaction when he'd used that word.

"Is it an anti-government group?" Hank asked.

"Anti-government, anti-everything. They're against anyone who's a different color or a different religion."

"A hate group," Hank said, writing the words in a notebook.

"Yes. Very militant. And they have my daughter!" Steven's face began to crumble as Olivia clutched his hand, but Olivia's own eyes held panic, too.

"I know this is hard, Mr. and Mrs. Landon, but we need to get all the information you can give us," Hank said. "How do you folks happen to be in charge of Leesa?"

Olivia took over. "We provide temporary shelter for foster children, kids who need a short-term place to stay until Social Services can provide a more permanent solution for their problems. We were called about Leesa because—"

"Everything's all my fault!" Leesa interrupted, starting to cry again. "It's because of me and Aaron, because we were…close. In school. And my father found out."

"The boy Aaron, who is Leesa's friend," Steven explained, "is Jewish."

Hank sighed and leaned back. His face showed that he understood.

"Aaron sent Leesa a note asking her to go out with him," Steven went on, "and Leesa's father found the note. The next day, after school, Leesa's father and brother ambushed Aaron and beat him badly."

Leesa buried her face in her hands and in a muffled voice added, "Then my dad locked me in my room and said I couldn't go back to school ever again."

Gently, as though he didn't want to press her too hard for fear of upsetting her more, Hank asked, "Where is your mother, Leesa?"

"She went away a long time ago. She couldn't stand living with The Unit. She wanted to take me with her, but my dad wouldn't let her. That was the first time he locked me up. I was five."

Jack felt his insides twist, both from fear over Ashley and from the awfulness of Leesa's story. No wonder she'd acted so quiet and remote. No wonder she'd shied away from him, trying not to even brush against him in the car—in spite of all that had happened, she was still in love with Aaron, according to what Ashley had told Jack. Or maybe "in love" was putting it too strongly; after all, Leesa was only a year older than he was. But with girls it was different, he guessed. Everyone was always telling him that girls matured faster than boys.

Hank asked, "Why do you think The Unit wants to get you back, Leesa?"

"Because the government took me away."

Olivia reminded her, "It was the Wyoming State Social Services that brought you to us, Leesa."

"They don't care. The Unit hates all government agencies—city or state or federal. If the government does something The Unit doesn't like, they try to get revenge."

The phone rang shrilly, making all of them jump. "Kodele here," the ranger said. "Yes. Yes. Keep them in sight. Have you contacted the California Highway Patrol and the Nye County Sheriff's Department?

Good. Everyone will stay right here until I hear further from you."

Returning the phone to its cradle, Hank told them, "They think they've spotted her. A ranger saw a pickup truck on the road to Furnace Creek with a young girl seated between two men. There was a rifle hanging in the back window of the truck cab. When the truck started to turn north at the Beatty cutoff, the ranger blocked it because he wanted to question the people inside, but they sped away."

"Which direction?" Steven asked.

"South, toward Furnace Creek."

Steven jumped up and said, "Then let's go after them!"

"Take it easy, Mr. Landon," Hank said. "The pickup truck will be under constant surveillance. We won't lose them, you can be sure of that. Before you could even get out of this building and into your car, the California Highway Patrol helicopter will be in the air, and it'll stay right above that pickup truck. The fugitives won't get away. As the saying goes, they can run, but they can't hide."

"I don't care, I want to be there," Steven demanded. "It's my daughter we're talking about!"

Placing his hands on Steven's shoulders, Hank guided him back into his chair and said, "This is a hostage situation, Mr. Landon, and we don't want anyone to make any foolish moves. For now all we want to do is observe the fugitives—no confrontations. Our main job is to get your daughter back safely."

"It's all right, Steven," Olivia murmured. As she laid her head on his shoulder, he put his arms around her, each of them trying to comfort the other.

Next to Jack, Leesa sat quietly crying. Maybe she was feeling guilty over what had happened, even though it wasn't her fault. If anybody was at fault, he thought, he was. Why hadn't he gone with Ashley and Leesa, instead of letting them wander off by themselves? Emotions churned inside him, making him wish he had someone to reach out to, someone he could tell how terrible he felt. He glanced at Leesa and cautiously placed his hand over hers. This time she didn't pull away.

"They've already done a license check on the pickup truck," Hank was saying. "I figured it would be registered to Leesa's father, but it isn't."

Steven told him, "Leesa's father and brother are in jail because Aaron's parents pressed charges against them. They were arrested for assault, and as far as I know, they haven't been released on bail."

Checking a computer screen, Hank said, "The truck is registered to a Robert Miller in San Bernardino County, California."

"California?" Steven repeated.

"The Unit has branches everywhere," Leesa told them. "They must have found out you were bringing me here, and they contacted the California branch. Those men wouldn't know what I look like, so they took Ashley by mistake."

"How would they have known who we were or where we went?" Olivia asked.

Steven answered, "Maybe someone spied on us at Furnace Creek last night. And followed us this morning."

The motorcycle, Jack thought.

Dabbing her eyes with the sleeve of her rumpled shirt, Leesa stood up to face Hank and said, "Take me to them. It's me they want. If I go with them, they'll release Ashley."

Like puppets pulled by the same string, all three adults shook their heads. Olivia brushed tears from her own eyes before she answered, "That's very brave of you, Leesa, but it's not a solution. We have to let the law-enforcement people handle this their own way." Then, after a pause, "Would you really want to go with them?"

"No!" Leesa wailed. "I don't want to go back to The Unit. I want to find my mother. But if they'd give Ashley back, I'd go with them."

Olivia hugged her then and patted her long dark hair, murmuring, "It will all work out." She didn't look as though she believed her own words.

The phone rang again, and this time Hank switched on the speaker phone so they all could hear what was being said. *Hank, this is Marvin reporting. The pickup truck turned off on the scenic loop road going to the old Harmony Borax Works—guess the driver thought it was a through road. When it petered out, he tried to drive across the dry lake bed, but the truck bogged down in the sand. Three occupants got out—two adult males and a young girl. Looks like the men are heavily armed. Right now they're walking into the desert."*

"Into the desert? Those idiots. Where do they think they're going to?"

"Beats me."

Hank barked, "How many law-enforcement people do you have?"

"We've got about a dozen from the Inyo County Sheriff's Department plus a SWAT team....Wait a minute!" The transmitted voice grew louder, more urgent. *"Hold on, Hank....It looks like one of the fugitives has opened fire on our officers! He's shooting at us. I count three...three shots!"*

"Don't fire back!" Hank yelled. "Keep them under surveillance but don't fire any weapons because of the child."

Olivia turned pale. As if to steady herself, she clutched the sides of her chair and closed her eyes.

"I've got to get out there!" Steven cried. "I won't try to do anything, but at least I want to be where it's happening."

"All right," Hank answered. "We'll all go. They've set up a new command post near the old Harmony

Borax Works. Leave your vehicle here, and we'll ride in the patrol car."

Inside the car, Leesa sat in the front seat with Hank so he could question her further about The Unit, while the three Landons (Jack hated the sound of that: the three Landons. There should have been four!) sat in back, too numb to even talk to one another.

Maybe it was because of nervousness, or maybe because in Hank, Leesa had found a father figure she could trust, but she began to talk almost nonstop.

"Mr. Kodele, you're part of the federal government, aren't you, because you're a National Park Service Ranger?"

"That's right."

"My dad says the federal government spies on us all the time. He says that when babies are born in hospitals, little microchips are implanted in them so the government can trace them and keep track of them all their lives. And that when you buy something at a supermarket, the bar codes tell the U.S. government what you bought."

"Now, why would the federal government care if I bought a bag of potato chips?" Hank asked her.

"I don't know," Leesa said, leaning back in her seat. "But I heard you talk about a helicopter that will keep surveillance on the pickup truck. Do you know about the black helicopters the government sends to spy on its citizens?"

"I've heard the rumors," Hank replied, "but they're not true."

Leesa sighed. "That's what Aaron says, too. He says almost everything my dad tells me is untrue—things like federal agents wanting Americans to register their guns so they can take them away and then we can't defend ourselves against government tyranny. Aaron says that's nothing but scare tactics and hate-group propaganda. He says that all my life, I've been fed a lot of lies, and I need to start learning the truth. Aaron is really smart. He reads everything, and he gets straight-A report cards."

"He sounds like a good kid," Hank said. "I'd like to meet him. Now I think I'd better pay attention to my driving here, because we're getting close to the turnoff point. We ought to be able to see the ground and air teams pretty soon."

As if Hank's words had conjured it, they heard the *thump, thump, thump* of a helicopter overhead. The turnoff to the Harmony Borax Mill had been blocked by wooden barriers, but a ranger moved one of them so Hank could drive through. Where the road turned into an unpaved, pebbly path, a dozen police cars and trucks were parked, while SWAT teams in desert camouflage uniforms grouped together, listening to their commander.

The Landons and Leesa scrambled out of the car to follow Hank toward a uniformed officer who seemed to be issuing orders. The man told Hank, "The fugitives are about two miles from here, out on the salt flats. They're heavily armed and very dangerous. You said they made their threat over a two-way radio. Do you have the radio that received that message?"

"Right here," Hank said, handing over the handset. "It belongs to the Landon boy—his name's Jack. He's the brother of the girl who's been abducted."

Abducted. The word made ripples of fear run down Jack's arms to his fingertips. He watched as the yellow-and-black handset, one half of his birthday present, was examined by the officer.

Calling one of the troops who was monitoring a group of communication devices, the officer said, "Sergeant, I want you to put fresh batteries in this two-way radio and find out what channel frequency it's tuned to. Then set up our systems to monitor that frequency. This may be the only method the fugitives have to communicate with us. Keep the line open—in fact, set up several lines on that frequency for backup."

"Yes, sir." As the sergeant walked away with the handset, Jack wondered what voice it would transmit next, praying it might be Ashley's, to prove she was unharmed. Whoever it was, he wouldn't hear it. Others were now in charge of his sister's life. Jack had no part in it—he was a useless bystander.

Hank had gone back to his police vehicle, where he was peering through a spotting scope mounted to the window on the driver's side. "I can hear a helicopter, but I can't see it," he murmured, and then he straightened up to stare at the sky. "No wonder I couldn't see it. It's flown two miles past where the fugitives are."

Sliding into the front seat of his police vehicle, Hank spoke into the radio to the helicopter pilot, "Hey, you need to drop elevation and come back. Turn right, and go west."

As Jack watched, the chopper flew lower, close above the desert's surface. It turned, as the pilot followed Hank's instructions to hover nearer to where the fugitives had been spotted. Since sound carries so clearly in the desert, the thumping of the helicopter's rotors echoed loudly in Jack's ears. He could also hear the pilot's voice, transmitted over the radio in Hank's vehicle.

Suddenly Jack heard something else, like the rattling of a marble in a can.

"They're firing on the chopper!" Hank cried.

Again came the sound of gunshots. Suddenly, against a background of bells and whistles going off inside the aircraft, the pilot's voice came over the radio loud and clear, shouting, *"Mayday, Mayday!"*

"They've been hit by gunfire!" Hank yelled. "The chopper's damaged!"

Like an injured bird, the helicopter dove and swooped as the pilot struggled to control it. Panic clawed at Jack's chest. If the chopper went down and exploded in the desert, Ashley could be hit!

In so many movies he'd seen, whenever a plane crashed, the fuel burst into a huge orange ball of fire. Anyone near that fireball would be killed. How close was Ashley to the damaged helicopter? he wondered. Right beneath it? If it crashed, if his sister died in the flames, the whole Landon family would be destroyed.

CHAPTER SIX

Half a dozen people were shouting all at once, "The crew wasn't hit, but the helicopter's disabled. Its oil line was severed. It can't fly."

Jack tried to run toward his parents, but the sergeant intercepted him, saying, "Things are getting tense here—you and that girl need to stay back out of the way."

"What's happening to the chopper?" voices were shouting. But no one seemed to know.

Jack pleaded, "My sister....Can't I go with my mom and dad?"

"Don't worry about them, kid, just do what I tell you," the sergeant demanded.

"But what about the helicopter?"

Just then a radio crackled, *"The chopper has landed safely. No casualties."*

Relief flooded Jack so strongly that he hardly noticed the sergeant instructing, "One of the rangers drove your Land Cruiser down here—it's parked near that fallen-down building over there. You two kids get inside the vehicle and stay there, hear?"

"Come on, Jack," Leesa said, taking Jack's hand.

The Cruiser stood so high off the ground that Leesa had to give a little hop to crawl into the backseat. That was good—the elevation gave them a better view of all the activity. Another helicopter had just taken off to pick up the stranded crew.

"The binoculars!" Jack said. "My parents left them in here. We can watch what's happening outside." He handed Leesa a pair and raised the other pair to his eyes.

It was impossible to see Ashley and her captors—they were a mile away on the desert sands, behind small hills, which is why helicopters were needed for surveillance. But Jack could follow the deployment of the SWAT teams being transported by truck. Sun reflected from the glass windows of the trucks, which had wide tires that could cross desert terrain without sinking in sand. At that distance, a shimmery desert mirage made it looks as though the trucks were riding on water rather than sand.

"Roll down the windows so we can hear, too," Leesa told him.

"I can't. They're electric windows. The motor has to be running before they'll work, and I don't know where the keys are. But I can open the tailgate." After he did, sound penetrated the Cruiser—people shouting, radios crackling, a fixed-wing Park Service Cessna flying low, right above them.

Uneasy, Jack and Leesa settled into the backseat. Jack supposed he ought to say something, but since nothing about this situation seemed real—it was more like a nightmare—no suitable words came into his head. All he could think about was Ashley, alone in the desert, captured by terrorists.

As if reading his mind, Leesa said, "Tell me about Ashley."

"What do you want to know?"

"Oh, just—who she is. I don't know her very well, and now I've gotten her into terrible danger...."

Jack answered, "Well, she's 11. She's in sixth grade. She has a lot of girlfriends, and...." What else could he say? "They're starting to get silly about boys and clothes and stuff."

Softly, Leesa said, "It must be nice, having so many friends. I was never allowed to have any unless their parents were part of The Unit." She lowered her head, twisting a damp tissue in her lap. "I went along with that until I met Aaron. At first I wouldn't even talk to him, because—well, because of what The Unit teaches us about Jewish people."

Jack was tempted to ask just what The Unit taught about Jewish people, but too much was happening outside. Through the powerful binoculars, he could see the crew from the damaged helicopter climbing into the rescue helicopter. Farther ahead, SWAT team members in desert camouflage moved forward, crouching down behind shields. Jack was so intent on watching them that he missed part of what Leesa was saying next; he didn't connect again until he heard, "Since I knew my dad would be away that night, I sneaked Aaron into my room."

"What?" Jack turned to stare at her.

"He wanted to find out how many cells The Unit has—you know, different branches—and where they are. I got the floppy disk with all the information, and I gave it to Aaron so he could copy it. He'd brought his laptop computer."

"What happened?" Jack could imagine Leesa's father breaking in and discovering the two of them together. Maybe that was when he'd beat up Aaron.

"Nothing happened. Aaron copied the disk and showed me the list of all the cells. That's how I knew there was one around here. They have a secret stockade at a place called Darwin Falls, right on the park boundary."

"Darwin Falls!" Jack exclaimed. "My mother said they found dead bighorn sheep near there. Why didn't you tell that to Hank when he was questioning us about The Unit?"

"I don't know. Do you think I should have?"

The Death Valley map lay crumpled in the tailgate; Jack reached over the seat to grab it. The place-names on the map were in such small type that it took him a long time to locate Darwin Falls. Then he said, "Look, Leesa. Here's Darwin Falls. It's not too far from Skidoo." His memory flashed back to the motorcycle rider who had stopped behind them on the road to Skidoo. What if he was one of *them?* What if he'd been spying on the Landons at Furnace Creek and had followed them? And when he saw them pull in at Skidoo, he notified the cell at Darwin Falls, and the men from there came and kidnapped Ashley.... Or maybe Jack was fantasizing the whole scene, playing it out in his head like a movie. "We at least ought to mention that to someone," he muttered to Leesa.

Staring through the window, she said, "I...I keep wondering if The Unit somehow found out that I let Aaron copy the disk. Maybe that's why they want me back. To punish me for betraying them."

"Punish you!" Jack exclaimed in alarm. "What would they do to you?"

"I'm not sure."

Just then the front door of the Cruiser opened and the sergeant got inside. "This operation is getting too big," he said. "We're moving the command post to the airport right behind Furnace Creek."

Jack had been so involved in his conversation with Leesa that he hadn't noticed how many cars and trucks had driven up the dirt road and parked. The vehicles were marked with a lot of different logos: Inyo County Sheriff; California Highway Patrol; Nye County Nevada Highway Patrol; Bureau of Land Management; and of course National Park Service.

"Where are my parents?" Jack asked. "I need to tell them something."

"They'll be driving down with Hank to the airport. Your mom asked me to take you two kids to a restaurant, and they'll meet you there."

"Did any messages come over my two-way radio?" Jack asked. "Did Ashley—?"

"Nothing. The kidnappers haven't spoken a word. What they've done is to dig a bunker out there in the sand, a hole deep enough for the two men and your sister to crouch down in." The sergeant started the engine. "Next they stacked up rocks in front of it for a barricade, but they won't need a barricade because we're not planning to shoot at them. Not as long as they've got your sister."

Poor Ashley, she must be terrified. And hot and thirsty—were they giving her any water? If the kidnappers didn't have much water, maybe they wouldn't give her any at all.

Jack began to study the map again. A narrow dirt road led from Darwin Falls to Route 190, the highway that went past Stovepipe Wells. What if other members of The Unit drove along that highway, then cut across the sand to the bunker where the kidnappers were holding Ashley? They could whisk her away and get back to their trucks before the law-enforcement people knew what was happening. Tracing his finger along the map, Jack could see how that would be possible. So maybe it wasn't that much of a fantasy.

"OK, kids, this is where you get out," the sergeant said, pulling to a stop in front of a restaurant called Wrangler Steakhouse. "Go in there and order whatever you want, your dad said, and charge it to the room. I'm taking this Cruiser to the command post at the airport hangar so your parents can drive it back here to meet you."

"How far is the airport from here?" Jack asked him.

"Oh heck, you could walk it easy from the visitor center. Look, I'm giving you this handheld radio; it's already turned on. You know how to operate one of these things, don't you?"

"Sure. I have one of my own," Jack answered.

"Good. If you have any questions or any problems, talk into it—we'll hear you. Anyone tries to talk to you, anything that doesn't look right, just yell into the radio. Now go on inside, the two of you, and get yourselves something to eat. Your folks will be here as soon as they can. Your mom said you haven't had anything since breakfast, and it's way past five."

The sergeant had already jumped out of the front seat and was holding open the back door for them.

The next thing Jack knew, he and Leesa were standing in front of the Wrangler Steakhouse. "Well, let's go in," he said.

The inside was noisy with the clatter of dishes and silverware, with the din of chatting diners, and over it all, a loud sound track of country-western music. Leesa looked apprehensively at the crowd of people waiting to be seated. Jack felt a little unsure of himself, too. He'd never before gone into a restaurant alone, escorting a girl.

"Party of two?" the hostess asked him. "It'll be about a 20-minute wait."

Stammering a little, Jack said, "That's OK. Nonsmoking, please. And could you take our names, and then we can go outside and come back here in 20 minutes? Would that be all right?"

"Sure," the hostess answered, picking up a clipboard.

After Jack spelled "Landon" for her, he turned to Leesa and said, "Come on."

"Where?"

"To check something." Jack wanted to find out exactly where the airport was located in relation to Furnace Creek Ranch, but when they walked around to the back of the restaurant, all they could see were the stables and housing for the ranch employees. "I know how we can figure out where it is," Jack said. "We'll just watch for helicopters coming and going."

The sky had turned crimson in the most spectacular sunset Jack had ever seen, but this wasn't the time to admire it. With his hand shielding his eyes, he looked overhead for aircraft, but only one flew past—far to the east and very high in the sky, a passenger jet headed for Las Vegas.

"I need to radio my parents," he told Leesa. "I want to tell them about Darwin Falls."

Since the radio was already turned on, Jack could hear commands crackling back and forth. Someone was saying, *"It'll be dark soon. Do all the ground forces have night goggles?"*

"Affirmative," another voice answered.

Jack was trying to figure out which button to press to send a message when Leesa mentioned, "Maybe we should go to back to the restaurant. I don't have a watch, but it feels like it's been about 20 minutes."

"You're probably right," Jack agreed. "Are you hungry? My stomach tells me I'm starved, but then I start thinking about Ashley, and I feel ashamed of being hungry."

The hostess seated them in a booth and handed them menus. Both Jack and Leesa studied the menus for a long time, checking out each item. A boy who didn't look too much older than Jack came to fill the water glasses, and then a woman stood beside their table, saying, "Hi, my name is Sharon, and I'll be your server tonight. Have you decided yet?"

Leesa's eyes slid from the menu to the woman as if she weren't sure what it was she was supposed to decide. Maybe she didn't eat in restaurants very often. Jack said, "I'll go first. I'll have the steak medium rare, french fries, and root beer."

"I'll have the same thing he's having," Leesa said.

"Soup or salad to go with that?" the server asked. Jack shook his head, no. Imitating him, Leesa shook her head, too.

Then they were alone, staring at each other across the table. Neither of them knew how to start a conversation in this very weird situation where they found themselves. Then, tentatively, Leesa began, "Before, when I asked you about Ashley, you didn't tell me much. There must be more. What's she like?"

Jack searched his mind, wondering what more he could say about Ashley—he'd never before tried to describe her to anyone. Images of his sister came into his mind: Ashley when she was five years old, wanting to tag along with Jack whenever he was playing with his own friends. Back then he'd thought of her as his pesty little sister. Many times he'd hidden from her, or sent her off to bring something from his room just to get rid of her, and when she came back, he'd be gone.

Ashley at eight, wobbling on her first pair of in-line skates, falling down but getting right back up, even though her shins were bleeding, wearing that stubborn look on her face that showed she was determined to master those skates. And she did.

Ashley the actress, learning fables and legends by heart, and then performing them for her family around a campfire, under skies where the Milky Way looked like a thick, dazzling carpet spread out above their heads. She could name all the constellations.

"Sometimes," Jack said slowly, "when Ashley doesn't know I'm watching, I'll see her take out one of her old Barbie dolls and just sit there holding it. It's like she wants to play with it, but she thinks she's too old now for Barbie dolls. She probably figures I'd make fun of her. So then she looks kind of sad, and after a while, she puts it away."

If they could only get Ashley back, Jack promised himself, he would save up all his allowance and buy her a *dozen* Barbie dolls! And he'd never tease her again for the rest of their lives. He bit his lip, feeling so awful inside that Leesa must have seen it in his face. On the sound track, a man was singing a mournful ballad about someone named Lucille, who'd picked the wrong time to leave him, with four hungry children and the crops in the field. "Those country-western songs always sound so sad," he murmured, making a lame excuse for his own gloom.

Leesa said, "Country-western was the only kind of music I ever listened to—before Aaron."

"Before Aaron?"

"Uh-huh." She seemed to fold into her memories, telling him, "Aaron has this CD player. He used to bring it to school, and when we started being friends, he'd play it for me—all this cool music I'd never heard before. My dad says rock music or reggae or salsa or hip-hop is all nonwhite music that comes out of a multicultural sewer. But when Aaron played it for me, I liked it. Not all of it, but a lot of it."

"Me, too," Jack told her.

"Then Aaron started teaching me other music, like songs by George Gershwin or Leonard Bernstein that I'd never been allowed to hear because they were written by Jews. And classical music by Stravinsky and Prokofiev and Shostakovich that my dad banned because he said those men were dirty communists."

Jack didn't know who some of those composers were, but he nodded as if he did.

"Aaron even taught me to dance. I didn't know how, because the kids in The Unit aren't allowed to go to school dances. Sometimes The Unit puts on dances for us, but all they play are country-western songs, because that's supposed to be the only uncorrupted white American music."

"Country-western isn't my favorite, but it's OK," Jack said. "There's a lot of it on the radio in Jackson Hole." That reminded him of the two-way radio the sergeant had given him, which was beside him on the seat. He hadn't been paying attention to anything that might have come over it because the restaurant was so noisy it was hard to hear. Picking up the handset, he turned the volume knob, but just then their steaks came.

Until he started eating, Jack hadn't realized how famished he was. Leesa just pushed her food around on her plate, spearing a few bites of steak with her fork, dipping a few fries in ketchup. She eyed Jack's empty plate and asked, "Would you like to finish mine? I'm not hungry."

"No thanks," Jack answered. He wouldn't have minded finishing Leesa's steak, but he figured it would be impolite.

When the server came to ask whether they wanted dessert, both of them said no, and Jack picked up the check. At the cash register, he said, "Uh, I was told to charge these two meals to my room."

This was a different hostess than the one who'd seated them. "Just sign your name and room number here at the bottom," she told him. When he did (after writing TIP $5 and hoping that was enough), she examined his signature and said, "You're Jack Landon? There was a phone call for you more than half an hour ago. I announced it over the intercom, but no one came."

"That must have been when we were outside," Leesa declared, looking at Jack.

"Was there any message?" Jack asked.

"Yes. From a Steven Landon—your father, I guess. He said he and your mother had been detained and you and Leesa are supposed to go straight to your rooms and lock the doors and wait there."

It upset Jack that he'd missed the chance to talk to his father, to find out what was going on, and to tell him about Darwin Falls. "Come on, Leesa," he said, and pushed ahead of her through the door.

Out here where it was quieter, he could contact his parents on the two-way radio the sergeant had given him. He studied it again, trying to figure out where the talk button was—the handset looked quite different from his own. It had a longer antenna, arrows pointing up and down like the volume on a remote control, and four buttons on the front marked P0, P1, P2, and P3.

"Jack, watch out!" Leesa yelled. She grabbed his arm and yanked him backward so hard that the radio flew out of his hand, right in front of the two-horse team pulling a buckboard wagon with a driver and three passengers.

"Hey, kid, pay attention. I nearly ran into you," the driver shouted.

At that moment one of the horse's hooves landed squarely on the radio handset. Jack tried to dive for it, but Leesa held him back. He watched in horror as the wagon's back wheel crunched the radio's antenna against the pavement.

"Oh my gosh! Now I'm *really* in trouble," he moaned. He'd just destroyed government property! Not intentionally, but what difference did it make whether it was intentional or not? His own two-way radio set had cost more than a hundred dollars; how much more would this far more complicated military radio cost to replace?

Fighting the temptation to close his eyes so he wouldn't have to see how badly the radio was wrecked, he dropped to his knees in the road. When a car approached, Leesa jumped in front of it and waved her arms to make it swerve around Jack.

"Pick up the pieces," Leesa told him. "Maybe we can find some glue and fix it." But from the expression on her face, he could tell she didn't really believe that.

CHAPTER SEVEN

The radio was in two pieces, held together by wires. All the way back to the room Jack tried to jam the pieces together. At the same time he wondered how many years he'd have to save his allowance, shovel snow in winter, rake leaves in autumn, mow lawns in summer, and get a paper route to pay for this wrecked bit of expensive military equipment.

"At least you didn't get hurt," Leesa told him. "You were heading right in front of that horse. It's better to have a broken radio than a broken leg."

Jack wasn't so sure.

The room he shared with his parents, 913, was right next to the one Leesa had shared with Ashley—915. "Like my dad said, lock your door when you get inside," he told Leesa. "Just in case."

"In case what?"

"In case that spy from The Unit might be hanging around—you know, the guy who followed us on the motorcycle? I mean, if he actually was a spy."

Jack watched to make sure that Leesa had entered her room and shut the door firmly, then he let himself into his own room and flopped onto the bed. What a terrible day! Could anything else go wrong? His only (very, very tiny) glimmer of hope was that his parents would be too upset about Ashley to worry much about the broken radio handset.

Swinging his legs over the side of the bed, he sat up and began to work on it again, manipulating the parts to see if he could fit them together. When the room phone rang shrilly, he jumped so hard the pieces flew out of his hands.

"Hello?" he said.

"Jack, it's Dad. Are you OK?"

"Uh...yeah." Jack hesitated, not wanting to blurt out just yet that he'd damaged an expensive military radio even though he knew he'd have to own up to it sooner or later.

"Is Leesa with you?"

"No, she's in her own room."

"Fine. Both of you stay put, do you hear? Your mom and I are still here at the hangar, and we won't be coming back to the room anytime soon. The kidnappers have started talking over the two-way radio that Ashley had with her."

"They have? What did they say, Dad?"

Steven spoke louder, raising his voice to be heard over the din of shouts and calls in the background. *"They asked for water to be dropped to them by helicopter."*

"Are they going to get it? Are the park people going to give them water?"

"No." The answer was curt, terse. *"They think that if they do, it will just make the standoff last a lot longer."*

Jack's mind raced. That meant Ashley would be suffering from thirst, even though the sun had gone down and the desert would be cooling off to night-time temperatures. He swallowed hard, imagining her thirst, wishing the law-enforcement people would just give in and send water.

"Jack, I want you and Leesa to keep your doors locked until we get there," Steven told him.

"OK, we will. Dad—" Jack was about to inform him about the cell of The Unit in Darwin Falls, when Steven broke in.

"Gotta go now. Something's happening here." There was a click, and then a dial tone.

Feeling useless for the hundredth time that day, Jack picked up the pieces of the radio and once again tried to fit them together. He was startled when he heard voices, faint but understandable.

"We've got things set up here for medical services,

plus there's a fire engine and a couple of ambulances."

"Yes, sir, and the two military helicopters from the California Highway Patrol are in the air now."

The two voices faded, then another voice came through loud and clear. *"Have one of the choppers drop a smoke bomb. We need to identify two things—the location of the fugitives and the direction of the wind. Tell the helicopter to fly high. I don't want another aircraft to get sniped at."*

"I'll convey that order, sir."

The radio couldn't be damaged too badly because Jack was still able to hear incoming messages. They were weak but audible. If he couldn't fix it, someone who knew more about electronics might be able to. Time passed—he wasn't sure just how much—before he heard another communique:

"Our troops are about 200 feet to the east of the kidnappers. We're moving forward in stealth mode, flat on the ground."

"Go to 150 feet and stop. No sudden movements. Remember—our strategy is to confine and contain."

Jack found the talk button and pressed it. "Anybody out there? Can anybody hear me?" but it wouldn't work—no surprise. "Rats!" he muttered. There was no way for him to send a radio message, and his dad hadn't given him a telephone number where he could reach the command post at the hangar. He tried to talk into the handset for a while longer, then gave up.

Stacked on the dresser were several Death Valley publications including another map, larger and more detailed than the one they'd had in the Cruiser.

Jack unfolded it and spread it out on the bed. He turned on every light in the room so he could read the map better.

For a long time he studied it, mulling over the worrisome idea he'd had when he was in the Cruiser. If members of The Unit had started out from Darwin Falls, they could drive along Route 190 past Stovepipe Wells, then park their vehicles off road and cross the desert on foot. Heading south, under cover of darkness, they might be able to reach the kidnappers. And coming from that direction, it was unlikely they'd be noticed by the SWAT teams, which were deployed to the east of the barricade where Ashley was being held prisoner. That much he'd learned from the short blasts of speech coming over the broken handset.

By now it was completely dark outside, so Jack thought he'd better close the drapes on the sliding glass doors that led to the patio outside his room. As he walked toward the doors his heart lurched. Someone was out there, looking through the glass at him. "Geez!" he yelled.

Scratching the glass with her fingernails, Leesa mouthed, "Let me in!"

Leesa! What was she doing out there on the patio? After rolling back the sliding door, Jack demanded,

"Why'd you come this way? You nearly scared the spit out of me. You could have knocked on the door from the hall, and I'd have let you in."

"I was going to, but when I looked through that little glass hole in my door, I saw a man standing there. Anyway, I wanted to talk to you first, so I came around the patio side."

"A man?" As Jack went to his own hall door and peered through the peephole, he wondered what she meant by "first"? Then he said, "There's no one there."

"There *was!*"

"I think you're just spooked," he told her.

Leesa took a deep breath. "I don't care whether you believe me about the man being in the hall, but I want you to listen to what I have to say. I've been thinking and thinking, rolling it around in my head ever since I got in my room...." She paused then, glancing nervously at him, appearing uncertain.

"And?" Jack prompted.

"I want to give myself up. To The Unit."

Now it was Jack's turn to take a deep breath. "Sit down," he told her, gesturing to one of the twin beds. He sat on the other one, facing her. "You already said that once to my mother, and she told you it wasn't an option. So why are you bringing it up again?"

The distance between the beds wasn't that large, and when Leesa leaned forward, her big, dark eyes stared straight into Jack's. "She's your parent, not mine. You have to do what she tells you, but I don't. If I go to the men who have Ashley, they'll let her go. They're not killers, they're not terrorists, they just have their own beliefs about how the U.S. government is destroying our way of life. If I turn myself over to them, they won't hurt Ashley. They'll just let her go, honest. I'm sure of that."

She made it sound so simple. Even reasonable. But it wasn't. "What are you planning to do?" he asked. "Just walk from here to the place where the kidnappers are barricaded in the desert? It's miles away, and it's dark outside. Even if you managed to hitch a ride with someone and you got as far as the Old Harmony Borax Works, the rangers would stop you. The road will be blocked off from that point on."

She got up and walked to the door. "I told you I saw a man in the hall." For a long minute she squinted through the peephole, having to stand on her toes because it was too high in the door, and she wasn't very tall. "They make these holes so that you can only see what's straight ahead of you, not what's on either side. But he's probably still out there." Turning again to face Jack, she said, "I think he's someone sent by The Unit. That's why I decided to give myself up. All I have to do is walk out this door and tell him I'm willing to go back."

Maybe Leesa was right, and that would solve everything, Jack thought. But should she be allowed to make that decision without any adults around? What would his parents say if she left after they'd been ordered to stay in their rooms? How was he going to stop her, if that's what she decided to do? He couldn't contact his parents on the broken two-way radio, and he didn't know how to reach them by phone. If Leesa opened his door right that minute and walked into the hall, what was he supposed to do—tackle her?

"I don't want you to go," he said.

"It's not up to you."

She was right. He had no right to interfere with her life. All he could do was try to persuade her. "Look, Leesa," he began, "you said those men aren't killers or terrorists. But your dad and your brother beat up Aaron pretty bad, didn't they? What if they'd killed him? I've heard about guys getting into fights where someone got knocked down and hit his head and died, and the guy who hit him was arrested for manslaughter. Even though it was just a fistfight."

Leesa stood with her hand on the doorknob, her eyes cast down.

"Just how bad was Aaron hurt, anyway?" he asked her.

"Pretty bad."

"And he got beat up just because he sent a note asking you to a movie."

She moved away from the door before answering, "There was more to it, but I don't know whether my father knew about it. One of the kids from The Unit who goes to my high school caught me with Aaron in the orchestra room. We were kissing." Moving across the room toward the dresser, she said, "Jack, I'm going to borrow your hooded sweatshirt, OK? It's chilly out there now, and I don't want to go back to my room for a sweater. I promise I'll return it."

"Wait a minute! Wait a minute!" Jack waved his hands. "Oh, I don't mean about the sweatshirt. Take it. But if you're going anywhere, I'm going with you. You can't run out into the night all by yourself." He didn't know why he was offering to do this when it would make him a collaborator in her crazy scheme. But he couldn't just let her fling herself into danger. Not all alone.

She frowned at him, then said, "I guess I can't stop you any more than you can stop me."

"Let me go first." Jack opened the door a crack to peer into the hall. If his dad knew what he was doing, Jack would be in the most major trouble of his life.

The part of the hall he could see through the crack looked empty. He inched the door a little wider. Behind him, Leesa reached out to push it, swinging it open all the way.

Nothing. There was no one in the hall.

"See? What did I tell you?" Jack asked. "It's your imagination. So come back in the room, and we'll lock the door."

Abruptly, Leesa said, "Forget that. You made a good suggestion in there when you said I could hitch a ride. If I can just get close enough to where they're keeping Ashley, I'll sneak past the rangers and run across the desert."

Grabbing her arm, Jack demanded, "Did you ever try to run through sand? I did, this afternoon. Your feet sink in, and it's hard to keep your balance. Believe me, you can't go fast enough out there to outrun anyone. And those law-enforcement people have big spotlights—do you think they won't see you? You'd get about 20 feet is all, and they'd catch you and bring you back. So what good would that do for Ashley?"

"Let me go, Jack." She said it quietly, but the look she gave him made him loosen his grip on her. It was a look he recognized—the same one Ashley had worn when she was determined to learn to skate. Stubbornness. Determination. That "nothing's going to stop me so get out of my way" look. "I have to do this," she insisted. "I couldn't stand it if Ashley got hurt because I just stayed here and didn't even try to help her."

Shaking herself free of him, Leesa started down the hall toward the double doors. Those doors led to the side of the motel, not the front, so there was no one Jack could turn to for help, no desk clerk who could tell him how to reach his parents at the hangar, and no guard who could demand that she stop. Nine o'clock at night, and everything was quiet as a tomb.

Until they pushed through the door. They'd barely reached the parking lot when a man's voice rang out from the shadows, "Leesa Sherman! Look over here!"

As the man came into full view, Jack saw that he was pointing something at them. "Leesa, drop!" he yelled. "He's got a gun!"

CHAPTER EIGHT

Not even thinking, moving entirely by instinct, Jack rolled over on the concrete and pulled Leesa with him to crouch behind a parked car. But the man kept coming—coming toward them. Jack tried to shield Leesa with his own body, but what good would that do if the man started shooting? They'd both be dead!

And then the man was standing right above them, shouting. Finally Jack's mind connected to what he was saying: "Hey, you guys, chill out. This isn't a gun. It's a camcorder."

Yeah, sure. Not believing, Jack stared at the shiny black object in the man's hand. In the dim light from above the motel door, all he could focus on was the dark circle that looked like the muzzle of a gun. It was pointed straight at Leesa. Jack was panting. Sweat stung his eyes. He knew—*he knew*—he was going to die. Several long seconds passed before his brain clicked in to what he was actually seeing—an object five inches high, four inches deep, one inch thick, with a gleaming round hole that was not the muzzle of a gun but happened to be the lens of a very small camcorder. Handheld. Hand-size. Jack had never seen anything like it.

Ignoring Jack, the man said, "Let me help you up, Leesa." He pulled her to her feet, brushing bits of dirt and tiny twigs from her back.

"How did you know I was Leesa?" she asked, trying to control her voice. She was shaking so hard it trembled. "And who are you?"

"I saw your picture on television. You were on the evening news. My name's Jesse Hererra—I'm a student at UNLV, the University of Nevada at Las Vegas."

"Wait a minute," Jack said. Pulling Leesa aside, he whispered into her ear, "Why should you believe him? He might be a member of The Unit."

"With a name like Jesse Hererra? No way," she whispered back. "He's a Latino—one of the so-called mongrels The Unit says are destroying the purity of the Aryan race."

Even though Jack knew that Leesa no longer believed that hate-group propaganda, the words still sounded shocking enough to make him cringe. "Well, if you're sure he's OK," he murmured.

"Look at him, Jack. He looks like Ricky Martin."

Jesse had pulled a card out of his wallet and was holding it in front of their eyes, even though in the dark they couldn't see much except a stamp-size photo of Jesse with his name underneath. "See, Jesse Hererra. I'm a TV reporter. This is my press card."

"I thought you said you were a student," Jack challenged him.

"I am. I'm a communications major at UNLV. Maybe I'm not all the way a full-time TV reporter, but I'm working on it. Look around you—do you see any other reporters? I was the only one smart enough to track down Leesa, and I recorded you guys on video tape. It'll make great footage with the two of you hitting the ground like you did."

"Hey, that's not fair!" Jack cried. "Are you going to show *that* on *TV?* I'll look stupid."

Leesa had been standing a little apart, eyeing Jesse. Now she moved forward and said, "That ID you just showed us—does that get you into places where other people can't go?"

"Yes. And I have a bigger press ID sign in my Jeep that I clip to the sun visor when I'm on my way to a story."

"Would it get you through police barricades?" she asked.

"Mmmm...." Jesse rubbed his chin. "Depends on how strict the cops are."

Taking Jesse's arm, Leesa said, "All right, Jesse Hererra, if you want a real story, get me through the barricades. On the way I'll tell you everything that happened. You'll have a real scoop."

Even in the dark Jack could see Jesse's eyes light up. "You got it!" he cried. "But I want an exclusive. No other reporters, right?"

Still suspicious, Jack asked, "Just who do you work for? Which television station?"

Jesse didn't answer that right away. Pointing to Jack, he said, "This guy must be Jack Landon, the brother of the girl who's been kidnapped, am I right?" When Leesa nodded, Jesse went on, "Well, actually, I don't really work for any particular station—I'm a freelance journalist. I get the story, and I sell it to the networks." Pointing to Jack, he asked, "Is he going with us?"

Leesa shrugged a little and replied, "You don't really need to, Jack. I'm all right now. I have a ride, so I won't have to hitch."

Jack couldn't believe the change that had come over Leesa. Hours ago, she'd been a weepy, scared girl full of guilt. Suddenly she'd become this take-charge action heroine like he saw on television shows, putting her trust in a stranger she'd met only five minutes before, telling Jack she didn't need him now. "I'm going with you," he announced. In this weird, surrealistic, nighttime scene, with a girl who'd been part of a hate group and a college kid who didn't look old enough to report anything scarier than a dog show, Jack felt like he was the only normal character with his head on straight. *Someone* had to keep touch with reality, and it appeared that job was going to fall on *him*.

They climbed into Jesse's Jeep, Leesa sitting in the front seat, and Jack pushing junk around in the back to find enough room for him to squeeze in. The floor was littered with empty soda cans. Other cans, full ones, rolled around, hitting Jack's feet when the Jeep started moving. An open sleeping bag hung over the back seat and trailed into the tailgate. Boxes full of notebooks and loose papers slid around in the tailgate. The Jeep smelled like pizza, which was no surprise since there were two smashed pizza cartons stuffed between the seats.

"Here, hold this," Jesse said, tossing the camcorder over the seat into Jack's hands.

That thing must have cost a ton of money! And there Jesse was, throwing it around like a candy bar. "So where are we going?" Jesse asked.

He meant the question to be for Leesa, but Jack answered. "Route 190. But we'll get stopped at the barricade at the old Harmony Borax Works, and that'll be the end of all this. Especially when the police see Leesa in here."

"So," Jesse said, glancing at Jack in the rearview mirror, "we shouldn't let them see Leesa. Or you."

Leesa seemed to be on the same page as this guy. "Jack and I will hide," she said. "We can scrunch down on the floor of the back seat while you talk your way through the barricade."

"That'll work. Hey, Jack," Jesse called to him, "look in one of those boxes back there. Find a baseball cap that says NBC, and in the same box you'll see a pair of glasses—they make me look older," he explained to Leesa.

"How old are you really?" she asked.

"Nineteen. I'm a freshman. But I've been doing this since I was 16. I've even had some stories on national TV."

"How many?" Jack wanted to know.

"Well, one so far. About a guy who claimed to have psychic powers. Said he could control the slot machines in Las Vegas with his thought waves. He really did seem to be able to. When I followed him around with my camcorder, he kept hitting one jackpot after another."

"And that story got on national TV?" Jack asked, unbelieving.

"Yeah. On *News of the Weird*."

Oh, great! Jack thought. "Let me ask you something. Is that a real press card you showed us?"

"It is. So's the one hanging from the visor. But I'll be honest with you—press cards like this aren't hard to get. You just join a certain freelance photographers organization and pay the very big dues they ask for, and they send you the card. So it's real, but it's not what you'd call major-league credentials. But it works. Some of the time."

What was Jesse getting them into? Leesa seemed intent on going ahead with her mission, putting her trust in this college kid, this would-be reporter, who would have to bluff his way to where she wanted to go. She started to talk to Jesse, telling him about everything that had happened from the time the Landons reached Skidoo. In a little while she stopped and said, "Slow down. We're coming to the turnoff."

"OK, Leesa, get in the back," Jesse told her. "Get on the floor and cover yourself and Jack with the sleeping bag."

"Wait a minute!" Jack said. "You don't even know where we're supposed to go if we do manage to get through the barricade."

"So tell me."

"OK." Jack was in this so deep already that he might as well play it out. "I have this theory," he said, "that other members of The Unit are planning to make a rescue attempt. I mean, it could happen." Jack had imagined the whole thing. "They could come from Darwin Falls and drive past Stovepipe Wells on Route 190, leave their vehicles, and strike out across the desert. Anyway," he added weakly, "that's my theory."

"Cool, dude," Jesse told him. "You be the navigator when we get past the checkpoint. Now, both of you better cover up for this undercover operation. That's a joke, guys, but do it."

Leesa quickly crawled into the backseat, then she and Jack started grabbing soda cans off the floor and throwing them into the cardboard boxes. "Don't you want your camcorder up there?" Jack asked Jesse. "If you're going to look like a reporter, you'll need it, won't you?"

"No. Give me that black press bag that's on the backseat next to the window. It's got bigger video equipment plus other cameras and rolls of film and tape. Hand over the tripod, too."

When Jack found the right bag, he saw that it was unzipped. A glance inside revealed equipment worth thousands of dollars, all jammed together helter-skelter without even any partitions to keep valuable cameras from banging into one another. Jack couldn't imagine that kind of carelessness—if his dad saw that, he'd blow a gasket. Jesse had to be incredibly rich not to care about how badly his cameras got hammered.

"What does your father do?" Jack asked him.

"He owns a casino and a couple of hotels, which is how I was able to find out where you were staying—through my hotel connections. So, give me the camera bag and cover yourselves with the sleeping bag. I see the barricade lights up ahead."

Like everything else in the Jeep, the sleeping bag smelled of pizza. Jack and Leesa pulled it over themselves as they flattened their bodies on the floor. When the Jeep stopped, they couldn't see anything, but they could clearly hear Jesse speaking to the officer who'd halted him. Jesse's voice sounded deeper now, more mature and very calm. "Good evening, officer."

"You can't go past here. This whole area has been cordoned off."

"I'm a member of the press corps, officer. I'm covering this story for national news. Here's my press pass."

There was silence. Jack could imagine the officer examining the card by flashlight, then turning the light on Jesse, who now happened to be wearing very serious-looking glasses and an NBC cap. "Where is it you want to go?" the officer asked.

"Just a little way up Route 190 so I can get a few shots for my network. If you or one of your men wants to accompany me, that would be fine. That would be great, in fact."

Jack sucked in his breath. What if the officer agreed?

"I can't spare anyone," the officer said. "All right. I'll give you ten minutes, but you can't go any farther than that little rise just ahead. That's all. Take your video shots and then get out of here."

"Thanks," Jesse said. The Jeep started to move again. As it lurched forward, Leesa's elbow bumped into Jack, but he knew better than to yell out.

"How much longer do you think we'll have to stay down here?" she whispered.

"Not too much longer, I hope," Jack muttered. "I'm suffocating."

His watch was not the kind that showed the time in the dark. After what he thought must be about five minutes—during which the Jeep never stopped moving—he cautiously moved the sleeping bag off his head.

"You guys OK back there?" Jesse asked. "You can get up now."

Jack gulped air, glad to be able to breathe again. "So what good is all this?" he asked. "I mean, we have to turn back right away, don't we? I heard the man say you could only stay for ten minutes."

"Yeah, that's what he said." Jesse kept driving, making no attempt to turn around. "So we're on Route 190—how far do we go?"

He wasn't going to turn back! Oh well—"Maybe about 15 miles," Jack answered. He wished he had the map—he hoped he was remembering it correctly. "We should stop a few miles before we get to Stovepipe Wells."

"And then what?"

Leesa leaned forward, her arms folded on the top of the passenger seat. "And then I'm going to walk across the desert to where Ashley is being held and ask them to let her go."

The Jeep swerved suddenly to the side of the road and slid to a stop. Turning around to face Leesa, Jesse asked, "You're going back to The Unit?"

She nodded. "Yes. You'll get your big scoop."

Taking off the baseball cap, Jesse smoothed his curly black hair. "I don't think I want a scoop that bad. Not just because I'll be prosecuted for letting you do that, Leesa, but because it sounds like the wrong thing to do."

So Jesse had a conscience after all. Maybe between the two of them, he and Jack could talk Leesa out of her crazy plan.

"Keep driving," Leesa told him. "Or if you don't want to, I'll just get out here."

Overhead, the thump of helicopter rotors started faint but grew louder and louder until the chopper was right above the Jeep. Then a bright spotlight shone down on them and an amplified voice ordered, "You in the Jeep. Turn around and go back."

Jesse stared long and hard at Leesa. "Tell me what to do, Leesa. If you want me to make a run for it in the Jeep, I'm willing. I don't think they'll shoot at us, and my dad will probably bail me out of jail."

Smiling at him, Leesa answered, "Let's do it then. Let's go."

CHAPTER NINE

Driving as though he thought he could actually outrace a helicopter, Jesse roared down Route 190 in the dark while Jack and Leesa clung to the handholds above the doors. All the while the chopper's bright searchlight beamed down on them, and the amplified voice kept telling them to stop immediately and give themselves up.

One thing was good—the light illuminated not only the Jeep, but the fringe of desert alongside the highway. Jack kept searching for trucks, for vehicles, for any sign that the Darwin Falls members of The Unit might have driven off road as a starting point for their ambush attempt. He was sitting directly behind Jesse, with his face pressed against the glass, because if the bad guys really were out there, they'd be on the left side of the road.

They'd gone no more than six miles when Jack yelled, "Wait, I see tire tracks!"

"So what?" Jesse shot back.

"They're fresh tracks. The wind hasn't blown them away. They might be from the guys we're looking for. Turn around, Jesse, and follow those tracks."

Jesse must have watched too many car chases in the movies, because he slammed the brakes so hard the Jeep spun out in a circle, throwing Jack and Leesa around like punching bags. Then Jesse jammed the gearshift forward and headed right into the desert. "Jack, take this camera pack," he ordered. "I have to pay attention to my driving, so I want you to get out the big video camera with the holding strap on top— see it? It's the best one for shooting in dim light."

Trying to keep his balance as the fast-moving vehicle bounced around, Jack reached over the seat to bring the heavy camera bag into the back. He had no trouble finding the video camera—it was the professional kind that had a great big lens and sat on a cameraman's shoulder. "Put it up here beside me," Jesse instructed, "so it's all ready to go when I need it."

Just as Jack dropped the video camera onto the front seat, they hit a bump in the sand that knocked him backward. Unconcerned, Jesse asked him, "Do you know how to work a camera?"

"Not a video camera, but I'm pretty good with prints or slides."

"Cool. Find yourself a camera in that bag. Each one is already loaded with film."

"You mean you want me to shoot pictures?"

"Sure. You'll be my backup photographer. I take video, you take stills."

Under safer circumstances, it would have been like getting turned loose in a candy store. Jack saw five cameras in the bag—he didn't know which one to pick, because they were all expensive cameras with the kind of fancy lenses even his father couldn't afford. He chose a Nikon with an 80–200mm zoom lens, but he had to hold onto it tightly because the wild ride kept getting bumpier, and he didn't want the Nikon to fly up against the ceiling of the Jeep and get smashed. He'd already ruined one piece of equipment that day, and that was enough.

"Hold on!" Jesse yelled, revving the engine as he tried to get traction on the desert floor. The Jeep sped up a little hillock of sand and then—they were airborne! They must have flown 12 feet before they hit the desert again with a bone-jarring bounce. Jesse gunned it, but the Jeep had had enough. Its tires dug into the sand and spun. The harder Jesse depressed the accelerator, the faster the tires spun, and the deeper they sank into the sand. That was it—they weren't going any farther.

"OK, everybody out!" Jesse ordered. "Jack, start shooting at anything that moves."

Since the helicopters qualified as moving items, Jack took pictures of them, but not when they were directly overhead because the downwash from the rotor blades practically blew him away. He covered the lens with his hand to protect it from all the blowing sand.

When the helicopter moved farther away and Jack was no longer caught in the downwash, he swivelled around to peer through his zoom lens at the desert sands. His spirits soared, because ahead on the sand sat three pickup trucks and two off-road vehicles, all parked randomly with their doors open, as though the occupants had jumped out of them fast. He'd been right! Someone—probably members of The Unit from Darwin Falls—had driven out into the desert, trying to connect with the kidnappers! About 200 yards straight ahead of him, through the zoom lens, he saw several moving shadows, but they were hard to interpret because the choppers' searchlights had not yet illuminated that part of the desert.

Amid the confusion of blowing sand, the noise from the helicopters, and the excitement of spotting the bad guys, Jack almost missed hearing Leesa. She was holding out her hand to him, shouting to be heard. "Good-bye, Jack. Thanks for everything. Tell your parents I'm doing this for them."

"Wait! What makes you think those guys are going to give up Ashley? Maybe they'll just keep both of you."

In the illumination from the Jeep's headlights, Leesa shrugged as she answered, "It's a chance I have to take. For Ashley." Then she turned away from him and began walking, a lone figure crossing the desert at night, heading into danger. He dropped the camera from his eyes to watch her. Leesa's long black braid swayed against Jack's red sweatshirt. From above, the helicopter's searchlight beamed down on her as if she were an actress on a stage, a tragic actress going forth to a destiny that no one could predict. He remembered her fear that The Unit might want to punish her, and a lump rose into his throat. Why hadn't he tried harder to stop her?

"Get pictures of her, Jack, get pictures," Jesse kept calling to him. With the video camera on his shoulder, Jesse was following Leesa's progress, then zooming in on the Darwin Falls cell members in the distance, then back to Leesa, and all the time he kept moving forward toward the action. Clicking his own shutter—but without much enthusiasm—Jack followed Jesse.

"Over there, Jack, over there!" Since his right hand operated the video camera, Jesse pointed with his left. Maybe the helicopter pilots had finally clued in on what Jesse was pointing to in the darkness, because suddenly one of the choppers dipped toward them and then veered away and up. Its searchlight picked out the militia members, eight of them, who were running bent almost double, holding automatic weapons in their hands.

Sweeping his own zoom lens in an arc, Jack thought he might be seeing something else farther away. Was it—yes. Maybe. The SWAT team! Uniformed men were crawling forward, coming closer to—to what? The barricade where Ashley was being held? Jack could barely make it out through the telephoto lens. "Don't miss any of this, Jack," Jesse kept yelling.

Forget it! Jack didn't care how many pictures he took with Jesse's Nikon. Jack's sister was out there, held prisoner by desperate men. "Here, take your camera," he told Jesse, thrusting the Nikon at him. "I'm going after Ashley."

He took off running as fast as he could, which wasn't very fast because of the sand. It was that same slow-motion nightmare all over again where he kept hoping he'd wake up and all the Landons would be safe at home at Jackson Hole. But this wasn't a nightmare, he was wide awake and terrified for his sister.

He didn't get very far before a man appeared like a ghost out of the shadows and caught hold of him. The man was dressed in a uniform of desert camouflage, but that didn't mean anything, because the bad guys as well as the good guys could show up wearing the same kind of uniform. His heart pounding in his ears, Jack cried, "Let me go! What do you want?"

"I'm SWAT team. Who the devil are you?"

"I'm Jack Landon," Jack yelled. "Ashley's my sister. I need to find her."

The man barked, "You're staying right where you are. What do you think you're doing out here anyway? This is a secure area. No civilians allowed." His grip on Jack's shoulders was so tight that Jack couldn't move forward at all, not even an inch. But he could see, because both helicopters were now beaming light on the action.

Everything seemed to be happening at once. The Darwin Falls men, all eight of them, moved closer to the barricaded dugout while the SWAT team stayed flat on the ground, less than 50 feet away. Under the blinding illumination of the searchlights, the whole thing looked like a scene from Hades. Figures dashed back and forth from shadow to light, light to shadow, with yells and shrieks punctuating the night. Jack strained to see the barricaded bunker, now in light, now in darkness. Where was Ashley?

"Throw down your weapons and surrender peacefully!" blared from one of the choppers. It sounded like the voice of God. "Throw down your weapons. You are surrounded." From the east crept another surge of SWAT team members. More from the north! If Jack and Jesse had kept going, they'd have bungled right into the teams of rescuers. "Drop your weapons! Drop your weapons!" the chopper's amplifier kept blasting. It was answered with a burst of gunfire as one of the militants raised his weapon and shot toward the helicopter. He must have missed, because the chopper pulled up a little higher and kept right on flying.

Suddenly the desert bloomed with flares. At that moment the eight men from Darwin Falls must have realized they were sitting ducks, that they were surrounded by troopers, police officers, sheriff's deputies, and SWAT team members, all holding rifles pointed toward them. "We give up, we give up!" they cried, their voices carrying clearly across the sands. Throwing down their assault weapons, they raised their hands in surrender.

Jack waited, his breath catching in his throat, as he stared intently toward the barricade where the actual kidnappers were hiding. After what seemed like an eternity, the two kidnappers climbed up out of their hole in the ground. They were waving white handkerchiefs over their heads.

But where was Ashley?

The SWAT team members began to move closer to the barricade the kidnappers had built, their rifles ready. Then, without warning, not more than 50 feet ahead of Jack, one of the kidnappers thrust his hand down as though reaching for a sidearm. "Duck!" cried the man who was holding Jack. He threw Jack onto the ground, out of the range of fire, but not before

Jack had seen two other SWAT team members pull Leesa down, too. Spitting sand out of his mouth, he jerked up his head. The kidnapper had frozen in mid-reach; he held his right hand immobilized, away from his holster, while he stared down at his chest.

Three red dots glowed on the front of the man's zippered jacket. Jack knew what that meant: He'd seen it at Yellowstone. The kidnapper knew what it meant, too. The three red dots were laser points, beamed from the sights of three separate rifles. If the man had pulled his handgun from its holster, even before he could have fired it, he would have been hit simultaneously by three bullets fired from three separate SWAT team rifles, each bullet hitting exactly where the red laser had pinpointed his jacket. Shaking, the man raised both hands into the air and yelled, "Don't shoot!"

"Please," Jack begged the man who was holding him, "let me go so I can find my sister."

"Take it easy," the man answered. "Our guys are working on it. This entire mission has been to get your sister back. We've caught all the men who were on their way to help the kidnappers escape, and it looks like both kidnappers have surrendered. Unless they're entirely stupid, they're not going to fight us when we move in to cuff them." He released Jack saying, "You don't have to lie flat anymore, but don't stand up. Just stay sitting."

By then, bright lights were sweeping all across the desert as though it were halftime at the Super Bowl. Some of the SWAT team members led the eight militia men away, jerking them forward by their elbows because their hands had been secured behind their backs. Others were patting down the two kidnappers, searching for weapons. Still others had jumped into the dugout behind the rock barricade. And then....

Jack let our a hoarse cry. There was Ashley, being lifted by the rangers. From that far away he couldn't get a really good look at her, but she seemed limp, as though she couldn't manage to stand up on her own. At the same time a helicopter was setting down very close to them. The men carrying Ashley ran toward the chopper, ducking low beneath the whirling rotor blades. When they handed Ashley inside, other waiting arms reached out to receive her.

The SWAT team member who'd been holding Jack spoke into his radio, "I've got the girl's brother here, too. Do you want me to bring him over so he can fly back with her?"

The answer cracked back into the handset. *"Sure. Bring him."*

"What about Leesa?" Jack asked anxiously. "Do they have room for Leesa, too?"

When the man relayed the question, the answer came back affirmative. He called over to the two

SWAT team members who were holding Leesa, and within seconds she and Jack were hustled across the sand toward the waiting helicopter.

"And Jesse," Jack wanted to know. "What's going to happen to Jesse?"

"You mean the guy who drove you out here?" When Jack nodded, the man said, "I think he's gonna be in a world of hurt."

CHAPTER TEN

Two o'clock in the morning, and all of them were still awake. They hovered around the bed where Ashley lay staring up at them, her eyes large, shadowed, and frightened—but no more frightened than Olivia's. Olivia held one of Ashley's hands, and Steven held the other, while Jack and Leesa stood at the foot of the bed.

"My throat hurts, Mom," Ashley said. "I was so thirsty."

"You're safe now, sweetie, and you can have all the water you want," Steven told her. "Or do you want juice? They have orange drink in the soda machine at the end of the hall—"

"No, don't leave, Daddy," Ashley begged him, looking fearful again.

"I'll get it," Jack offered, and Leesa said, "I'll go with you," but Ashley stopped them with, "I don't want any of you to go away from me right now. For such a long time I thought maybe I'd never see you again, so now that we're all together, I want you to stay here with me. Please?"

Steven knelt beside the bed and gently stroked a tangle of her curls. "You've been through a terrible ordeal, Ashley. But you're safe now. We're here."

Ashley closed her eyes, but didn't quit talking. "The one man kept staring at me and staring at me, and he wouldn't stop, and I got so scared. Then he said he had a daughter just my age, and he was feeling bad about everything they were putting me through. But when I asked him for water, he said there wasn't enough, and he had to save it for himself and the other man. He wouldn't give me any."

"Did either of them try to hurt you?" Steven asked, his grip tightening on Ashley's hand.

"No. When they found out they had the wrong girl, they were mad at first, but not at me. They kept yelling at each other about how stupid the other one was. And that's what really worried me because they had so many guns—the guns were standing up against the sides of the dugout where we were hiding, and some were lying on the ground. I wasn't afraid they were going to shoot me, but I thought they might try to shoot each other, and I'd be in the way."

Olivia sat on the bed and put her arms around Ashley. "It's all over now. No more guns."

They decided that Jack and Steven would share one room while Leesa would stay with Ashley and Olivia. "Can I sleep in your bed with you?" Ashley asked her mother, sounding so pathetic that any of them would have agreed to anything she asked for.

"Of course," Olivia answered. "Now, if Jack and your dad will leave us and go to their own room, we three ladies can get ourselves tucked in for the night."

"Please keep the door open—the one between the two rooms," Ashley begged. "If I can hear Daddy snoring, then I'll know he's right there."

"Who, me?" Smiling for the first time in 15 hours, Steven protested, "I don't snore. I bet you'll hear Jack snoring, not me. He snores up a storm."

"I do not snore," Jack said, glad they were making a joke, no matter how feeble it sounded. Ever since Ashley's rescue, their emotions had been running so deep, so painful, that even that silly bit of banter brought relief, especially when he saw a tiny smile curl the corners of Ashley's lips.

"I'm supposed to meet with the park people tomorrow to talk about the bighorn sheep," Olivia said gently. "Would you like me to cancel, Ashley? Because if you'd like me to, I will."

Ashley shook her head no. "Every time I close my eyes I see those bad people and their guns. I need to think about other things. Can I go with you? That will help me think about sheep instead of kidnappers."

"Of course you can come. We'll all stick together from now on."

Sheep. Darwin Falls. Jack remembered that there was some kind of connection, but he was too tired to call it to mind. It would probably come back to him in the morning.

#

The next thing Jack became aware of was a pounding on the door of the room. "Huh? What time is it?" he asked, groggy, and then remembered that he was wearing his wristwatch. "It's nine in the morning. Are you awake, Dad?"

"I am now. Who the heck is banging on the door like that?" Steven hurried out of bed, pulled on his jeans, and opened the door to the hall.

Jesse stood there, leaning against the door frame, grinning. "Rise and shine," he greeted them. In one hand he held two capped, insulated mugs inscribed "Death Valley National Park" and decorated with Indian symbols. In the other hand he balanced a cardboard tray holding three Styrofoam cups. "Hot coffee for the grownups, orange juice for the kids," he announced, breezing past Steven. "At your service."

Jack let his eyes roam over Jesse from his curly black hair to his Kenneth Cole loafers. He was dressed in tan cargo pants with a brown leather jacket and a pale green crew shirt that accentuated his dark good looks. Everything about him seemed expensive—and careless, as though none of it mattered to him. Clean-shaven, bright-eyed, energetic, he might have just come from a spa rather than a harrowing nighttime raid in the desert. Jack and Steven, on the other hand, looked as though they'd been dragged across the sand by coyotes.

"I just came to say good-bye," Jesse told them, gingerly setting the orange juice onto the dresser. "I have a two-o'clock class, and before that, I want to drop off my videotape at the national network news office." He patted the pocket of his jacket, where he was carrying the tape. "Thanks to Jack and Leesa, I've got a winner here. It'll be on the six-o'clock news for sure. National news! I thought you might want to watch."

"I'm not interested in your kind of journalism. You led these kids into danger for the sake of a story," Steven said, cold anger in his voice.

Jesse waved his hands in the air. "Whoa, whoa, whoa! I plead not guilty to that charge, Mr. Landon. Look, man, you can ask Jack. If I hadn't given Leesa a ride, she was ready to hitch, and that would have been a whole lot more dangerous. You never know who might have picked her up in the dark."

Pulling a T-shirt over his chest as if it were armor, Steven answered, "That's no excuse—I know why you did what you did. You had a thousand other options, and you chose to film the story for your own gain. You showed an appalling lack of judgment that put my son and Leesa and Ashley into danger. I think you'd better go." Steven planted his feet into the carpet like tree roots, his arms crossed so tightly that his biceps bulged beneath the sleeves of his T-shirt. He kept his eyes on Jesse, like a cat tracking a mouse.

"Well, I'm sorry you feel that way, Mr. Landon," Jesse said finally. "I know I might have gone a little over the line—"

"A *little?*"

"But I didn't make Leesa do anything. It was her choice. She wanted to!"

"What Leesa did or did not want to do is irrelevant. She is a child. You are an adult, or at least claim to be. You should have stopped her."

For a moment Jack stood there, his face closed off as his mind went reeling. The accusation against Jesse—those words of condemnation belonged to *him,* Jack Landon. Only Jack had been aware of Leesa's plan right from the beginning. Only he had agreed to the bargain being struck—Leesa for Ashley. Had he been wrong? It had all worked out, with everyone safe, and yet...the words his father hurled at Jesse were true for Jack as well. It could have worked out a thousand different ways, many of them perilous. He'd been lucky.

"Dad," Jack said softly, "It's not Jesse. The whole thing was my fault."

"What?"

Jack squared his shoulders. *"I'm* the one who knew about Leesa's plan. *I'm* the one who didn't stop her. I didn't know what to do—I just wanted Ashley back."

"It's OK, Jack." Leesa had come to the still-open door connecting the two rooms. She stood there half hidden, looking tousled in a long sleep shirt. Her hair stuck out in wisps, full of static. Olivia hovered just behind Leesa.

"It was my decision, Mr. Landon," Leesa stated. "Don't blame either one of these guys. For the first time since I can remember, *I* made a decision about what I thought was right. And I'm not sorry."

Steven didn't seem to know what to say. Olivia looked just as puzzled, probably because they'd never before heard Leesa stand up and state her own convictions. The anger that had set Steven's face into a hard mask seemed to soften as he nodded at Leesa. As the tension lessened, Jack felt himself let out the breath he'd been holding.

"How'd you get out of jail?" Leesa suddenly asked Jesse.

Jesse's cocky grin returned as he answered, "No jail time so far. They're still trying to figure out what laws I might have broken—the only ones they're sure of are that I was speeding out there on Route 190 and that I drove a vehicle off the paved road, which is a big no-no. As for being there in the first place—I had permission, remember? The ranger allowed me to go through the checkpoint. Anyway, my dad has a whole slew of his lawyers already working on this—"

He left it dangling. As Jesse stood there, looking happy with himself, Jack was glad nothing bad was going to happen to him. Jesse might be a wild card, but Jack liked him and would never forget their adventure together. Jesse was probably going to make a great television correspondent, barreling his way into wherever the action was, tramping down all the barriers, doing anything necessary to get his story. Maybe all first-class newsmen were like that.

Jesse continued, "The thing is, Leesa, because of your attempt to give yourself up, the SWAT team captured eight conspirators from Darwin Falls. They didn't even know those Unit guys were out there until we drove into the desert after them."

"Is that true?" Steven demanded.

Jesse shrugged. "It's what the police told me. If we hadn't got there when we did, those eight guys might have reached the kidnappers, and who knows what would have happened then? It could have turned into a real bad shootout—with Ashley caught in the middle."

Leesa walked over and gave Jesse a little hug.

"Hey, what's that for?" he asked. When Leesa didn't answer, Jesse looked down at her, his lips turned up in a warm, crooked smile. "Hey, Leesa," he said, "about five years from now, if you break up with Aaron, give me a jingle. You won't have any trouble finding me—I ought to be famous by then."

"I believe that," she answered. "Thanks. For everything." Jack didn't know whether she was thanking Jesse for the ride into the desert, for the invitation to look him up in five years, or for the orange juice. Or all of the above. Jack crowded beside her to shake Jesse's hand. Jesse was a way cool guy.

"See you, people," Jesse said, backing into the hall. "Gotta get this tape to the network news, plus, like I said, I have a two-o'clock class." With that, he was gone, and it seemed to Jack as if the energy level of the room had dropped considerably.

"Well," Steven said, looking at Olivia.

"Well," Olivia echoed. "What a way to start the morning." Before they could even close the door, a motel employee approached them waving a white envelope. *"Es la señora*—is Olivia Landon?" the woman asked in a strong Spanish accent.

"That's me," Olivia said, taking the envelope from the woman and saying, *"Gracias, señora."* After she opened the envelope and scanned the contents, she announced, "It's from Hank Kodele. He'd like me to come to his office whenever we can. So— let's get dressed."

"You want all of us to go?" Steven asked.

"I don't know if I ever want to leave the kids

again," Olivia answered. "Maybe sometime I will, but for now, humor me." Turning to the girls, she said, "I get the shower first."

"Leave the door open," Ashley said sharply. "At least a little bit, Mom. And maybe sing like you do sometimes. I need to be sure you're there."

Where did Ashley think Olivia could go? There wasn't even a window in the bathroom. It seemed that Ashley had been so traumatized by her ordeal that she had to make sure each of her loved ones was near her—to see them or touch them or just hear them.

"I'll sing your favorite song from when you were little," Olivia told her gently. "'Let the Sunshine In.' Do you remember?"

Jack remembered. His mother had sung that to him, too.

CHAPTER ELEVEN

An hour later, Jack stared out the window as their Cruiser rolled past the visitor center and along Route 190 once again. In the daylight the highway looked ordinary and innocent, with all traces of last night's drama removed from sight. The sand had been blown smooth, as if nothing more than gusts of wind could polish away trauma. As Jack watched the mountain peaks blend into the horizon, he thought about what he had admitted in the motel room, to his parents and to himself.

He'd made a decision to help Leesa. Listening to his father rail against Jesse for his irresponsibility, Jack realized how much his own decision could have cost them all. But it had worked out, he argued with himself. He had his sister back safely, and that was all that mattered. And yet, he couldn't help wonder if success was the only criterion for justifying a judgment call. Was anything he did OK as long as it worked out all right? Or were his choices like prints left in sand…the outcome could blow one way or another, depending on the nature of the wind.

A tumbleweed skittered along the side of the road. Jack sighed and watched it grow smaller, until it disappeared like a dot behind him. Maybe he'd have to grow old before things came clear to him. Or maybe some questions just didn't have any good answers.

When they reached the law-enforcement headquarters and found the right office, Hank waved them inside. His reading glasses dangled against his chest, held in place by one earpiece stuck into his uniform pocket. The stark white of his T-shirt made a *V* at the base of his tanned neck. Square-faced and muscular, Hank managed to appear both serious and friendly. "How's our girl today?" he asked.

"Trying to recover from her fright," Steven answered. "It's going to take a long time."

Ashley did look haggard. Though she'd bathed and washed the sand out of her hair, she still had a pallor beneath her sunburn. "I'm OK," she told Hank.

"You're a tough little lady. Those men who had you were pretty rough guys." Hank leaned across his desk to pick up some papers and raise them toward the Landons. "Our folks have been busy this morning," he began, pulling out his reading glasses and putting them on. "We've found out a great deal about the kidnappers. They belong to that chapter of The Unit at Darwin Falls, part of the same cell as those other eight men who were on their way to help them." He riffled the papers, saying, "Although the men live in different towns around here, even as far away as San Bernardino, they've built a hideout right on the park boundary. It's a little shack where they hold meetings. Our people located the hideout early this morning. What we found there was pretty interesting."

Hank looked up then to ask, "Do you folks know what's just across the Death Valley National Park boundary, on the west side?"

When they answered no, he told them, "It's the China Lake Naval Air Weapons Station. It covers about a million acres, and it's where they test such things as guided missiles and rockets and all kinds of shelled explosives. They shoot 'em into this vast empty place to see if they work, which most of them do. But some of them blow up accidentally." Glancing at them, he added, "And there are others that *don't* work right then, but they don't blow up either. They just land and lie there."

Jack began to wonder what all this was leading to.

"It's such an enormous area," Hank said, "that it's impossible to patrol the whole thing. So there are a lot of unexploded weapons and pieces of weapons and guided missile systems lying around. It's illegal for anyone to go in there and pick anything up, but some people do. We call them 'scrappers' because they take all the scrap they can find."

"What kind of scrap?" Steven asked.

"Oh, aluminum, wire, steel—I'm not sure what all of it is. The naval base hires legal contractors to go in and clean up the stuff, but too often the illegal scrappers get to it first. But the stuff I just mentioned is pretty minor." Hank moved around to sit on the front of his desk, facing them. "What the scrappers are really hoping to find are the unexploded missiles or munitions. There's a huge black market for military weapons, and the prices paid for them are high. *Very* high."

"And that's what these men were doing?" Olivia asked. "Selling unexploded munitions?"

"You got it. The papers we found in their hideout tell it all—that's what I'm holding here: Copies of those papers. The Unit made a mint by selling this stuff to terrorist groups, but that's not all they were into. No siree." Suddenly Hank reached behind him to pick up chunks of something Jack couldn't identify.

"Know what this is?" Hank asked. "Jack? Leesa? Ashley? Want to guess?"

He handed a piece to each of them.

Oddly shaped, the pieces looked like hunks of dark brown rubber. Those Hank gave to Leesa and Ashley were no bigger than tennis balls, but the one he gave to Jack was the size of a thick book. Jack tried to bend it, and it gave a little but not much.

"A new kind of Play-Doh?" Ashley ventured.

"One of those balls that you squeeze to strengthen your grip?" Leesa guessed.

Jack turned his piece over in his hands, studying it. Finally he admitted, "I'm clueless. What is it?"

Hank laughed and picked up another piece from his desk. "This," he announced, "is solid rocket fuel. This is what fires the boosters that put the space shuttle into orbit. It's also used to make defense missiles. When there's a test-firing accident at China Lake and a missile blows up before it takes off into the air, pieces like this fly all over the place."

"I get it," Jack said. "I bet The Unit tries to sell this stuff on the black market to terrorists who want to blow up things."

Rubbing his hand across the weathered skin of his cheek, Hank answered, "Close, but not quite. This stuff won't work unless it's contained and fired from inside a rocket casing." He dropped the piece on the table, where it bounced just a little. "See? No explosion. But here's what it *will* do." From a drawer, Hank pulled out a Swiss army knife and opened one of the blades. Then he carved a slice from the rocket fuel, the way he'd cut cheese from a chunk of cheddar. "Now watch this," he said. "All of you better stand back."

On his desk sat a wide, metal ashtray. After placing the slice of rocket fuel in the center of the tray, Hank opened a book of matches, struck one, and held the match to the small, brown, rubbery cube.

A flame shot up so high and so suddenly that Hank had to leap out of the way. "Wow! That stuff would be great for starting campfires," Jack yelled.

"Right. It won't explode, but it sure burns like crazy. That's why those militia guys were collecting it," Hank said.

"To make campfires?"

"No, folks. For arson. Imagine putting a bunch of this stuff into a church or synagogue and setting it on fire—it would go up like tinder. The Unit had a lot of plans to commit arson. Catching them last night not only saved some buildings, it also potentially saved lives."

Olivia reached to take the piece from Jack's hand and examine it. "You say you found a lot of larger fragments like this just lying around on the ground at The Unit's campsite?" she asked Hank. "Do you know what rocket fuel is made of?"

"Can't even guess," he answered. "I'm no chemist."

"Neither am I, but maybe we could call someone at China Lake and ask them," she suggested. "I'm very curious, but for another reason."

"Why don't you just look it up on the Internet?" Steven suggested. "You can find almost anything on the Net. May we use your computer, Hank?"

With a sweeping motion, Hank pulled back his chair and pointed to his screen. "Be my guest."

Within five minutes they had their answer. By weight, solid rocket fuel was made of 69.6 percent ammonium perchlorate; 16 percent aluminum in particle size (very fine like flour); 12 percent polymer; and small amounts of iron oxide, plus a curing agent.

"Ammonium perchlorate," Olivia murmured. "That's an inorganic salt, very soluble. I've read reports about water contaminated with that stuff—it sickened rabbits and rodents that drank the water. Damaged their thyroid glands."

"The pieces weren't anywhere near water, so they couldn't have contaminated anything," Hank told her. "They were just stacked on the ground. I mean, some of them were stacked. Others looked like they'd been knocked over by a wild animal. What are you getting at, Dr. Landon?"

Again Olivia stared at the piece in her hand. Then her eyes opened wide.

"You said the stack was knocked over?"

"Yes."

"How big was the stack?"

Hank held his hand off the floor. "About yay high—a couple of feet. Why?"

"It would have been a large animal that knocked it over. "

"Probably—"

"Did you see any tracks?"

"Can't say I looked for them—but now that you mention it, that is near the area where the sheep turned up dead."

"A salt lick!" she exclaimed.

"Huh?" No one was sure what Olivia meant.

"You know how ranchers put out blocks of salt for cattle to lick?" Olivia asked excitedly. "If the bighorn sheep came across these hunks of rocket fuel made of 70 percent ammonium perchlorate—an inorganic salt—and they licked them, it could make them very sick—or even kill them, because they'd be getting it in an almost pure state rather than diluted by water."

Ashley cried, "Congratulations, Mom! Sounds like you solved the mystery of the sheep deaths."

"It's too soon to be sure," Olivia demurred, shaking her head. "We'll have to do a lot more investigation and analysis. But it's a starting point, and that's more than we've had so far, since the blood test I was waiting for came back marked 'inconclusive.' This really could be it!"

"Well, one thing *is* sure," Hank said. "Sheep are a lot like little kids. They'll take a taste of anything they find lying around."

"That sounds just like my brother, Jack," Ashley announced. "I've seen him eat things a lot grosser than ammonia whatever-that-was. Once a long time ago, he found this old piece of—"

"Hey—don't tell that story!" Jack protested. "I was just a kid!"

"So? Anyway, Jack found this disgusting stuff stuck on his—"

"Wait! I'm sure Hank doesn't want to hear this story," Jack insisted.

"No, no," Hank said, smiling broadly. "I don't mind. Go ahead, Ashley."

"Yeah, Ashley, keep talking," Leesa instructed. "This sounds like something I want to hear."

"It does," Steven agreed, at the same time Olivia pressed her fingertips into her forehead and murmured, "I'm not sure it's anything *I* really want to know." To Hank, she added, "As the kids get older, I keep learning about mischief I never discovered back when it actually happened."

As Ashley went through the embarrassing story, animating every detail so that everyone laughed, Jack only pretended to care. Inside, he knew what it really meant. Ashley was coming back to her old self. She might still have a long way to go, but she'd taken the first step. He had his sister again.

CHAPTER TWELVE

I think this is a very special reward for us," Olivia announced.

The four Landons and Leesa were still sitting in the Cruiser, parked to the east of the steep Panamint Range. The sides of the mountains had been sculpted into wide canyons that descended as much as a thousand feet per mile, from halfway beneath the peaks all the way down to the alkali flats. It was in those cool, green canyons that the wild burros hid.

"Reward, Mom?" Ashley asked. "For what?"

"You're mother's being modest, as usual," Steven said. "What she means is that it's pretty unusual for the Park Service to allow civilians like us to witness a wild burro roundup. They're letting us do it as a special reward because your mother figured out what was wrong with the bighorn sheep."

"I figured it out—perhaps," Olivia corrected him. "We won't know for sure until more tests are run. That's the scientific method: Test and confirm, and then test again to make sure." Looking up at Steven, she added, "And what I really meant was that just being here—all of us—on this beautiful day, surrounded by mountains with the pink glow of dawn on their peaks…well, it's the kind of reward life hands you sometimes. You have to feel grateful."

Smiling back at her, Steven touched her cheek and said, "You're sounding pretty philosophical for so early in the morning."

"Can we get out of the Cruiser?" Jack asked, impatient with all the talk. The wild-burro roundup would be starting soon. He could see the four wranglers riding back and forth, warming up their horses. The burros would be herded by helicopter until they came close enough to a V-shaped catch-pen corral that had been assembled out of metal pipes. Then the wranglers would take over, chasing the burros, one at a time, and forcing them inside the corral. And after that the ground crew—two men and a woman who were now sitting on the rails of the corral—would get to do their jobs of guarding the gate so the captured burros couldn't escape again.

"I guess we can get out of the Cruiser," Steven was saying, "but we'll have to keep well out of the way when the burros get here. You wouldn't want to get run over by a burro. Or by a horse. I guarantee you it doesn't feel very good."

"I know. Remember, I nearly got trampled by that wild mustang near Zion National Park," Ashley said. "Did you ever get run over by a horse when you were at the boys ranch for foster kids, Dad?"

Steven raised his eyebrows and gave a wry grin. "Nothing as scary as what happened to you at Zion, but my feet got stepped on by horses plenty of times. Believe me, when a horse is standing on you, you can't move. You just try to keep from bawling in front of the other guys while you wonder how many bones are getting broken in your foot."

By then, all five of them had left the Cruiser and were moving toward a little hillock. From there they could see everything, but still be far enough away that they wouldn't interfere with the roundup.

"You were a foster kid, Mr. Landon?" Leesa asked.

"I was. It gave me some of the best and some of the worst experiences of my life. But I made it through."

"And you turned out just great," Olivia said, taking his hand and swinging it. "Let's sit here on the sand. And Leesa, I think it's OK now for you to let Jack and Ashley in on your big secret."

"What secret?" they both asked.

Leesa gave them the biggest smile Jack had seen on her face since she'd come to stay with the Landons. "It's about my mother. She's coming to get me. She was watching the national news and saw the story about me—the one Jesse videotaped! So she called right away, and she's on her way from Milwaukee. She should be here tonight, and I'll go home with her. I'm so happy."

"To Milwaukee? Wisconsin?" Ashley asked. "You'll be so far away! And what about Aaron?"

Leesa's smile dimmed a little. "Aaron and I will stay in touch. Letters and e-mail and phone calls. Some day...." She left it unfinished.

Soft in the distance, but growing louder, came the thud of a helicopter, a sound Jack would never have trouble recognizing for the rest of his life, since he'd heard so much of it during Ashley's abduction.

"Do you have the binoculars?" Steven asked.

"Got 'em," Jack answered.

Steven didn't need the binoculars; he was peering through the big telephoto lens he'd attached to his camera. "Looks like the pilot is driving the burros down that canyon over there," he said, pointing. "You three kids can take turns watching for them. Yell when you see them."

Jack expected the wranglers to ride their horses to where the burros would be appearing, but instead they stayed near the catch-pen corral. "Why aren't the wranglers moving out, Mom?" he asked.

Olivia explained, "Those burros are smart. They know how to pace themselves when they're running so they don't get too tired. They can keep going for a long time, back and forth, back and forth. Since the helicopter will be herding first one group of burros, then another group, then another one, all day—"

"Will this really last all day?" Leesa interrupted.

"I expect so," said Olivia. "That's why the wranglers don't chase the burros over a wide area across the desert flats—they're trying to spare their horses. They let the helicopter do the chasing."

Anxious, Leesa asked, "Will we be back in time to meet my mother?"

"Don't you worry about that," Steven said, giving Leesa's braid a reassuring tug. "We'll get to the motel in plenty of time before your mother arrives."

"I see them, I see the burros," Ashley cried as she stared through the binoculars. "What long ears they have! They look like junior-size horses that have been crossed with jackrabbits."

Soon the burros moved close enough that Jack could follow them without the binoculars. Running in single file, heads held high, were four adult burros and one little one. "Oh, look at the baby!" Ashley enthused. "Isn't it cute?"

"A baby burro is called a foal," Jack told her. "And the females are called jennies and the males are called jacks. But I don't know how you can tell which is which from this far away."

"With the binoculars," Olivia answered. "The light-colored one is the jack."

"Just like you, Jack," Ashley joked. "Now I know why Mom and Dad named you Jack. It's because you're light colored, you've got big ears, and you're a donkey brain!"

He had a smart-aleck comeback on the tip of his tongue, but he held it in. Let Ashley tease him as much as she wanted—he didn't care. She'd been returned safely to her family, and that was all that mattered. He was glad she felt good enough now to make fun of something, even if it was her big brother.

Olivia was right about the burros: The energetic little beasts ran back and forth, determined to escape. Right behind them, the helicopter pilot kept swooping, trying to herd them in the direction of the catch-pen corral, flying low enough that they surely must have felt the downdraft. Suddenly one of the burros reversed field like a football player, ducking beneath the chopper to head back toward the hills.

"Way to go, jenny," Ashley yelled.

"How do you know it's a jenny?" Jack demanded.

"'Cause it's too smart to be a jack," she giggled.

The pilot kept after the burros, making one pass after another, until finally he got all of them close to the corral. Then the wranglers took over. Swinging their lariats, each of the four wranglers started out after a different burro, one on one.

"They won't have to rope the foal," Steven said. "It will follow its mother."

Bucking and swerving, the four burros managed to escape the lariats until the pursuing horses had worked themselves into a lather, but still the wranglers kept after them. Dust rose from the desert floor; the wranglers whooped and hollered; the horses whinnied and the burros brayed. The valiant fight lasted a long time before the burros succumbed to the skill of the riders. One after the other, the burros were herded to the wings of the corral, which acted like a funnel into the corral itself. The frightened little foal trotted after its mother, just as Steven said it would.

Soon the pandemonium inside the corral grew wilder than the chaos outside. The two men and one woman who made up the ground crew clung to the railing to keep an eye on the burros, ready to intervene if the animals hurt each other or the foal. After all five burros had been driven into the corral, the gate was slammed shut, and the wranglers had a few minutes to catch their breaths before the helicopter brought in the next bunch of animals. The burros ran around the inside of the pen, squealing and braying.

"I *hate* this!" Ashley exclaimed vehemently.

"Honey, what's wrong?" Olivia asked.

"I know how they feel, locked up like that, scared to death because they don't know what's going to happen to them. They've been kidnapped by strangers just like I was."

Putting his arms around her, Steven said, "It isn't the same, Ashley. These animals are being captured to save their lives. They'll be adopted by people who will take good care of them and learn to love them."

Ashley hid her face against her father's chest. "I still hate it."

It was Leesa who seemed to know what to say. Taking Ashley's hand, she told her, "You're right, Ashley, it's scary to lose everything you've been used to. But sometimes it can be a good thing."

When Ashley raised her head, Leesa went on, "I'll tell you the truth—I'm scared, too, because everything is changing for me. I haven't seen my mother since I was five years old. But I have to believe I'm trading my old life for something that will be better."

Ashley whispered, "You're so brave, Leesa. I wish I could be like you."

Taking a deep breath, Steven said, "Maybe we've had enough of the burro roundup for today. I've shot lots of film, so let's get back to the motel and start packing up for our trip home. Tomorrow Leesa will start her new life…."

"And the rest of us will get back to our old one," Jack said. "You know what I'm going to buy you for a coming-home present, Ashley?"

"What?" she asked.

"A Helicopter Barbie. So you'll always remember how you were lifted out of the valley of death."

"You're weird, Jack," Ashley said. Smiling, she added, "But I guess we'll keep you."

AFTERWORD

Death Valley, in spite of its name, is a land of life. It is also a land of self-discovery, where people have been able to live their lives free from the restraints of more populated areas. The boom-and-bust cycle of desert mining is one of the most colorful parts of Death Valley's past. Silver, gold, copper, borax, and other minerals were mined well into the 20th century, by "single-blanket jackass prospectors" and by large mining companies. The mine at Skidoo, mentioned in *Valley of Death,* produced more than a million dollars before the hardships of desert mining forced it to close.

Death Valley National Park is part of the Mojave and Colorado Deserts Biosphere Reserve. Its plant and animal communities thrive in a variety of life zones, ranging from a vast salt pan on the valley floor to bristlecone pine forests at the higher elevations. Nearly

500 vertebrate species, including the endangered desert tortoise and the Devils Hole pupfish, have adapted to the extreme conditions.

The coyote is one of my favorites. This wily predator has gained respect for its intelligence, hunting skills, and ability to adapt to the steady increase of humans. Olivia's observation that it's a "bad, bad situation when wild animals become dependent on handouts" is especially true in the case of this charming desert "song dog." Coyotes often run alongside roads looking for an easy meal. Visitors who stop to feed them often forget that they are dealing with wild animals and are bitten. Then park officials must remove or—in extreme cases—kill the coyote. Educating people about the importance of letting wild animals find their own food is an ongoing activity.

Desert bighorn sheep are a different story. They are so shy that it is a rare treat even for park rangers to see one. So, when sheep die, it makes us worry about the population's long-term well-being. The sheep deaths that Olivia is asked to investigate still have not been explained, but they do not appear to have been caused by disease or any unnatural event. But we carefully monitor these animals and will keep our eyes open for bogus "salt licks!"

What we *are* sure of is the impact the activities of feral burros have had on native desert bighorn sheep. This furry little beast arrived in the area with the earliest gold seekers, serving as their beasts of burden and companions. When the boom times ended, the burros were left behind to fend for themselves—and multiply. These voracious plant-eaters destroyed native plant communities, polluted waterholes, trampled stream banks, and eroded hillsides with their criss-cross paths. The native sheep population, unable to compete with the burros for food and water, began to move out. To prevent an ecological disaster, park managers started the burro roundup program.

It really was a treat for the Landons and Leesa to witness a roundup. The complex logistics of using wranglers and helicopters to corral the burros and trucks to remove them from the park make it impossible to open these events to the public. Roundups, which usually take place twice a year, are done with the utmost care and with as little stress to the animals as possible. After the roundup, the burros are given to the Bureau of Land Management or to a private animal rescue group for adoption. This program has led to the creation of a more productive and ecologically sound environment for the bighorn sheep and other native species. This, in turn, helps insure that future generations will be able to enjoy the extraordinary natural wonders of Death Valley National Park.

Linda W. Greene
Chief, Division of Resources Management
Death Valley National Park

SNEAK PREVIEW—

Follow the Landons as they travel to
Virgin Islands National Park in

ESCAPE FROM FEAR
MYSTERY #9

Like a ghost ship, the boat drew closer and closer until it came to rest about 20 feet from shore, where it dropped anchor. Half a dozen dark shapes leaped out of the boat and started toward the beach.

"Poachers!" Steven cried under his breath. But the dark shadows paid no attention to the nesting turtle; instead they ran straight for the trees, disappearing into the inky blackness, shadows into shadow.

"What should we do—where's the flashlight?" Olivia cried. In the darkness, as Steven fumbled to connect his flash attachment to his camera, four more dark shapes ran past them, melting into the trees.

Two other people—both men—had jumped out of the boat and waded to shore, heading straight for the turtle. "Give me a hand with this—it's heavy," one man said, bending over to get a hold of the turtle's shell.

"What 'bout dem eggs?" the other man asked.

"We'll get them next. I love the smell of turtle—smells just like money!"

The men grunted as they lifted the turtle as high as their knees. With bowed backs, they began to make their way toward their wooden vessel.

"They're taking her! Stop! Leave her here!" Olivia shouted, leaping up from the blanket.

"Mom, wait! Those men might have guns!" Ashley screamed. In a flash she was beside her mother, with Steven right behind, grabbing Olivia's arm.

Wrenching her arm free, Olivia cried, "We can't just watch—they'll kill her for the shell!"

Alerted by her cries, the poachers started to run. Curses rained down as they splashed toward the boat, the turtle swinging wildly between them. Jack knew this turtle would die. If the men threw her on the boat, they would wrench the shell from her back and kill her and all the eggs she was still carrying. Taking a step forward, he felt the flashlight beneath his shoe. The light. If he could catch them in the flashlight's beam, he'd be able to see the registration number on the boat and give it to the authorities. In an instant he scooped up the flashlight and fumbled for the switch. His hands felt as stiff as if they'd been held under cold water— why wouldn't his fingers work right? The flashlight tumbled from his hands to the ground, but when he grabbed it once more and commanded himself to calm down, he located the switch and turned it on.

The beam cut the night like a saber. He knew the poachers would flee like cockroaches rather than let anyone get a good look at their faces. But the moment he tried to aim the beam at them, he felt something hit him from behind.

"What!?!" Jack stammered. He took a step but found himself reeling—a poacher must have found him, knocking him onto his back. He felt a vise-like grip as a hand attempted to pry the flashlight from his fingers. Then Jack caught a flash of a face in the beam. Forrest. It was Forrest, trying with all his might to wrestle the light away.

"Give...it...to...me!" Forest said between gritted teeth. He was strong, but Jack punched him with an elbow, rolling free in the cool sand. Forrest fell onto his back but was up on his feet as fast as lighting, lunging once again at Jack. *"Give it up!"* he grunted. Driving at Jack's middle, he pushed him to the ground, landing on top of him with a thud. They flipped, one over the other, and Jack felt his flesh scraping against tree root. Forrest had gone crazy. Nothing made sense.

As Jack fought back, the flashlight beam bounced crazily through the trees where a half dozen dark forms were running straight up the rocky hillside toward North Shore Road. In that wildly swinging beam, Jack saw one face that he recognized without a doubt....

To find out who Jack recognized and what happens next, look for ESCAPE FROM FEAR *in July 2002.*

To read samples from the other mysteries in this series go to Gloria Skurzynski's Web site:
http://gloriabooks.com/national.html

DON'T MISS—

WOLF STALKER
MYSTERY #1
Fast-paced adventure has the Landons on the trail
of a wounded wolf in Yellowstone National Park.

CLIFF-HANGER
MYSTERY #2
Jack's desire to help the headstrong Lucky Deal
brings him face-to-face with a hungry cougar in
Mesa Verde National Park.

DEADLY WATERS
MYSTERY #3
Jack and Ashley's efforts to save an injured manatee
involve them in a thrilling chase through the Everglades.

RAGE OF FIRE
MYSTERY #4
In this tale of myth and mystery, a Vietnamese orphan
named Danny leads Ashley and Jack into a steaming
crater in Hawaii Volcanoes National Park.

THE HUNTED
MYSTERY #5
While attempting to help a young Mexican runaway, Jack
and Ashley flee for their lives from an enraged mother
grizzly in Glacier National Park.

GHOST HORSES
MYSTERY #6
Life-threatening accidents plague the Landons as they
investigate the mysterious deaths of some white mustangs
on a trip to Zion National Park.

OVER THE EDGE
MYSTERY #7
Jack relies on high-tech cyber skills to find out who is
threatening his mother after she broadcasts her plan to
save the condors in Grand Canyon National Park.

ABOUT THE AUTHORS

An award-winning mystery writer and an award-winning science writer—who are also mother and daughter—are working together on Mysteries in Our National Parks!

Alane (Lanie) Ferguson's first mystery, *Show Me the Evidence,* won the Edgar Award, given by the Mystery Writers of America.

Gloria Skurzynski's *Almost the Real Thing* won the American Institute of Physics Science Writing Award.

Lanie lives in Elizabeth, Colorado. Gloria lives in Boise, Idaho. To work together on a novel, they connect by phone, fax, and e-mail and "often forget which one of us wrote a particular line."

Gloria's e-mail: gloriabooks@qwest.net
Her Web site: http://gloriabooks.com
Lanie's e-mail: aferguson@sprynet.com
Her Web site: http://alaneferguson.com